Sólo por ti

Peggy Moreland

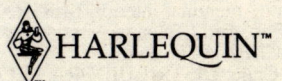

Editado por HARLEQUIN IBÉRICA, S.A.
Núñez de Balboa, 56
28001 Madrid

© 2008 Peggy Bozeman Moreland. Todos los derechos reservados.
SÓLO POR TI, N.º 1628 - 24.12.08
Título original: The Texan's Contested Claim
Publicada originalmente por Silhouette® Books

Todos los derechos están reservados incluidos los de reproducción, total o parcial. Esta edición ha sido publicada con permiso de Harlequin Enterprises II BV.
Todos los personajes de este libro son ficticios. Cualquier parecido con alguna persona, viva o muerta, es pura coincidencia.
® Harlequin, Harlequin Deseo y logotipo Harlequin son marcas registradas por Harlequin Books S.A
® y ™ son marcas registradas por Harlequin Enterprises Limited y sus filiales, utilizadas con licencia. Las marcas que lleven ® están registradas en la Oficina Española de Patentes y Marcas y en otros países.

I.S.B.N.: 978-84-671-6655-2
Depósito legal: B-43839-2008
Editor responsable: Luis Pugni
Preimpresión y fotomecánica: M.T. Color & Diseño, S.L.
C/. Colquide, 6 portal 2 - 3º H. 28230 Las Rozas (Madrid)
Impresión y encuadernación: LITOGRAFÍA ROSÉS, S.A.
C/. Energía, 11. 08850 Gavá (Barcelona)
Fecha impresion para Argentina: 22.6.09
Distribuidor exclusivo para España: LOGISTA
Distribuidor para México: CODIPLYRSA
Distribuidores para Argentina: interior, BERTRAN, S.A.C. Vélez Sársfield, 1950. Cap. Fed./ Buenos Aires y Gran Buenos Aires, VACCARO SÁNCHEZ y Cía, S.A.
Distribuidor para Chile: DISTRIBUIDORA ALFA, S.A.

DESTINY UNKNOWN

MARIS SOULE

BANTAM BOOKS
NEW YORK · TORONTO · LONDON · SYDNEY · AUCKLAND

DESTINY UNKNOWN
A Bantam Book / February 1997

LOVESWEPT and the wave design are registered trademarks of Bantam Books, a division of Bantam Doubleday Dell Publishing Group, Inc. Registered in U.S. Patent and Trademark Office and elsewhere.

All rights reserved.
Copyright © 1997 by Maris Soule.
Cover photo copyright © 1997 by Mort Engel Productions.
Floral border by Lori Nelson Field.
No part of this book may be reproduced or transmitted in any form or by any means, electronic or mechanical, including photocopying, recording, or by any information storage and retrieval system, without permission in writing from the publisher.
For information address: Bantam Books.

If you purchased this book without a cover you should be aware that this book is stolen property. It was reported as "unsold and destroyed" to the publisher and neither the author nor the publisher has received any payment for this "stripped book."

ISBN 0-553-44530-8

Published simultaneously in the United States and Canada

Bantam Books are published by Bantam Books, a division of Bantam Doubleday Dell Publishing Group, Inc. Its trademark, consisting of the words "Bantam Books" and the portrayal of a rooster, is Registered in U.S. Patent and Trademark Office and in other countries. Marca Registrada. Bantam Books, 1540 Broadway, New York, New York 10036.

My thanks to Karen Berger, Diana Fox, Caroll Drudy, and Susan Carrigan for their assistance with this book.

Dear Reader,

In my previous book, *Destiny Strikes Twice*, both Effie Sanders, the heroine, and her sister Bernadette were struggling with their careers and their love lives. Effie's destiny was changed by Parker Morgan, but that left Bernadette, and she was too fascinating a person for me to ignore. She was also a problem. I could identify with Effie (at least in some ways), but Bernadette wasn't a bit like me. Oh, I admire tall, beautiful women who dress immaculately and are in complete control of their emotions; it's just not in my nature to look that perfect. When I was a child, my mother would French-braid my hair, scrub my face, and send me off to school in a pretty dress. By the time I got home, half of my hair was hanging down around my face, and I had dirt on my knees and a tear in my dress.

Maybe it's because I'm not like Bernadette that I decided to throw her into a situation where she would lose some of that control and have to look beyond the external to find true love. As a child, I'd heard the story "The Golden Chain." It says so well what I believe and what Bernadette had to learn: that the real value of a person is in what he or she is, not in outward appearances. "The Golden Chain" was what Bernadette needed—or a man with a golden chain. Enter Cody Taylor.

Ah yes, I love fairy tales . . . and dogs . . . and a little mystery. Mix them all togehter, and I had another story begging to be told.

Maris Soule

PROLOGUE

Effie opened the door, and Bernadette Sanders knew one day of marriage hadn't changed her sister. Effie was still a redheaded pixie, full of energy and bounce. She welcomed Bernadette into the apartment with a wave of her hand and a question. "Did you get Dad off okay?"

Scraping the snow from the soles of her boots, Bernadette stepped inside. "As we speak, he's on his way to Pittsburgh. From there, it's JFK, and by tomorrow he'll be back in Cairo."

"I still don't understand why he left so soon. I thought he was going to spend a few days with you."

"You know Dad." Not that Bernadette herself professed to understand their father and his constant need to be digging up the past. "Those ancient artifacts were calling."

A movement down the hallway caught Bernadette's attention. She glanced in that direction and watched a tall, good-looking man walk toward them, a small, long-haired dog prancing at his feet. Fourteen years earlier

2

Parker Morgan had been her boyfriend. Now he was her brother-in-law. Life was indeed strange.

"Believe it or not, I think we're ready," Parker said, and lay his overcoat on the largest of the four suitcases sitting in the hallway.

Bern nodded toward the luggage. "Sure you two don't want me to drive you to the airport? I really do think we could fit those into my car."

Parker shook his head and positioned himself beside Effie. "My wife wants to ride in a limo, so we're going in a limo. To some unknown destination, for six weeks of—"

"Pure sex," Effie finished, scooping up the dog. Mischief glinted in her green eyes when she looked at Bern. "One thing I can assure you, he's not going to be anywhere near Grand Rapids or a telephone. This time he's truly taking a vacation."

Bernadette understood. The last vacation Parker had taken, he'd spent almost as much time at his two department stores in Grand Rapids as he had at his Gun Lake cottage. Not that the vacation hadn't changed his life. In those two weeks he'd hired Bernadette to be the general manager for his stores and had proposed marriage to her sister. Both Bern and Effie knew, however, that the only way to make Parker relax and forget the stores was to get him out of the country and away from telephones. Bernadette had some numbers Effie had given her in case of a dire emergency. Otherwise, she was on her own for the next six weeks.

She looked at Parker. "Any last-minute instructions, boss?"

He shook his head. "You've been my general manager for seven months now. You know the job. And Ben will help you."

Destiny Unknown

3

Bernadette wasn't sure how much Benjamin Waite would help. After all, she had taken his job. She did know that she had to show Parker she could manage things on her own. "We'll get along fine."

He grinned. "Knowing you, you've just been waiting to get me out of your hair."

Bernadette said nothing, but he wasn't far from right. She had been waiting. For sixteen of her thirty-one years—ever since Parker's father had kiddingly said that if she studied hard, he'd make her a manager in one of his stores—she'd wanted to be in this position. Now she was manager of both branches of Morgan's Department Stores, and for the next six weeks, she would be virtually the boss.

"And will I even recognize the stores when I get back?" Parker asked, grinning.

"I'm not making that many changes." In her office she had a chart showing the proposed changes to be made over the next six months, all approved by Parker. Starting Monday she would be getting in touch with contractors regarding the remodeling. Loren McVeigh, Morgan's art director, was already working on a Web site for the Internet, and the ads and window designs for spring would reflect the family-oriented atmosphere they wanted to stress.

Everything was under control, exactly as Bernadette liked it.

"I'm worried," Effie said, snuggling her face close to her dog's. "I've never left Mopsy for more than a few hours. She's either been with me at the shop or been performing with me when I did my clown act. Would you mind taking her with you to work?" She glanced up at Parker. "At least for a few days, until she gets used to me being gone?"

Parker's shrug said he didn't care, and Bernadette knew how much Effie loved her dog. Leaving Mopsy for six weeks would be like leaving a child. "No problem," she said. "Auntie Bern will take good care of her niece."

Subj: *Once Upon a Time*
Date: *97-02-22 19:47:33 EST*
From: *Morgans*
To: *Troll*

The King and Queen have left the kingdom, and woe be to the Golden Princess. All I promised, I have done. What should have been, now will be.

ONE

Monday morning, only three hours after arriving at the downtown store, Bernadette sat behind her desk, Mopsy on her lap. In silence she stared at the two sponges Benjamin Waite had placed on her desk. As far as she could tell, they were exactly the same. Identical in size, color, and texture. Identical in manufacturer.

Ben spoke first. "One of these will absorb liquids, the other won't."

Reaching over the dog, Bern picked up the two sponges. They felt the same. The synthetic material was as close a match to living sponge as she'd ever encountered, which was why she'd talked Parker and the buyer for housewares into stocking them in the stores. "Which one will absorb and which one won't?"

"That's the problem. You can't tell until you use them."

Since both sponges had a corner cut off, Bern had a feeling Ben knew the answer. He opened the plastic container he'd brought with him, and Mopsy lifted her head, her button nose sniffing.

"This is some chicken soup my wife made," Ben said. "I think it will illustrate the problem."

Ben dipped the two sponges into the container, and Bern watched as one sponge absorbed the soup and the other didn't. He was right. They had a problem. "How many have been sold?"

"Not that many. We didn't get these on the floor until Saturday, but we've had two returned this morning."

"I want to see the shipment." She stood, setting Mopsy on the floor, then pushed in her chair and started for the door. Mopsy trotted after her, but Bern stopped the dog. It was one thing to bring Mopsy to the store so that she didn't get lonely, another to have the dog running loose. Carefully she closed Mopsy into the office.

They were on their way to Shipping and Receiving when Ben stopped. "Dang it all! I forgot the original purchase order. It's on your desk. I'll just be a minute."

True to his word, he was back by her side in a minute. Five minutes after that, they were in Shipping and Receiving, looking at sponges. "So, what do we do?" Ben asked.

For Bern the decision was easy. She wasn't going to waste valuable time having her employees check which sponges would and which would not absorb liquids. "Send them back. All of them."

She signed the order and, as long as she was in the area, took time to go over incoming and outgoing shipments for the day. She also stopped by the lingerie department and talked to the two clerks there. Lingerie was not doing well this month, in spite of Valentine's Day. The clerks had reported missing inventory, and sales were down. Something was wrong.

In all, no more than a half hour had passed from the

time she'd left her office until she returned. Nevertheless, the moment she opened her door, Bern knew she had a problem.

Ben's plastic soup container lay on the carpet, a grease stain showing where some of the soup had soaked in. Beside the stain lay a sponge. And beside that stood Mopsy, legs spread and head down.

When Mopsy choked up a shredded portion of sponge, Bern knew what had happened. The dog had gotten on the desk, knocked the container of soup onto the floor, and gobbled up the soup. Once that was gone, she'd eaten the one sponge that had absorbed the soup.

Going to Mopsy, Bern knelt beside her. Though she'd called herself Mopsy's aunt from the time Effie had gotten the dog, she knew nothing about dogs. Should she pick her up and shake her? Thump her on the back? The Heimlich maneuver didn't seem reasonable, not on a twelve-pound mop of hair, but Bern tried. Putting her hands around the dog's ribs, she squeezed.

The dog choked even harder.

"Oh my gosh. What happened?"

Bernadette turned at the sound of the voice. Anne Closson, administrative secretary to Parker for over eleven years and to his father for several years before that, stood in the doorway, her gaze on Mopsy. "She got into some soup Ben brought," Bern said. "He'd dipped a sponge into it, and she ate that too."

Once again Mopsy gagged. Anne didn't hesitate, but headed back to her desk. "I'll call a vet."

Of course, a veterinarian. Bern chided herself for not thinking of that. If a child were choking, you called a doctor. For a dog, it was a vet.

She gave up on the Heimlich maneuver. Mopsy was in misery, her sides straining and the look in her eyes pained, but she was breathing. Shaking, thumping, or squeezing might cause more harm than good.

Effie had said Mopsy would eat anything, and Bern knew the dog could jump as high as a chair. Why hadn't she pushed in her chair? She usually did.

What had she said to Effie? *Auntie Bern will take good care of her niece.* Well, Auntie Bern wasn't doing such a hot job at the moment. "Please," she begged as Mopsy gagged up another piece of sponge. "Don't die."

"I found a vet who will see you right away," Anne said, coming back into the office. She handed Bern a slip of paper with a veterinarian's name and address. "His clinic is located just down the road. The receptionist said he's spaying a dog at the moment, but he should be done by the time you arrive."

Bernadette had never been in a veterinarian's office. With Mopsy tucked under her arm, she pushed open the door and stepped inside.

The waiting room was lined with empty chairs, and there were magazines spread out on end tables. A receptionist was stationed behind a high counter. On first impression it wasn't unlike a medical doctor's office. Then again, from the smells surrounding her to the noises coming from the back room, it was very different. Behind one closed door there was incessant barking. Behind another, mournful meowing.

And from behind a third door a man yelled. The barking stopped, but not the mournful meowing.

"That is one unhappy cat."

Bern looked at the woman who had spoken. The receptionist was probably in her mid-twenties, could use a

Destiny Unknown

good hair styling and some makeup to enhance her features, but was reasonably attractive.

"I'll be glad when the owners come get him," she went on, smiling. "Are you the one who called? The one with the dog that swallowed a sponge?"

"It was my secretary who called." Bern stepped up to the counter, relieved to have reached help. "I left the soup and sponge on my desk. I didn't think she could get to it."

The receptionist stood and leaned over the counter for a better look at Mopsy. "Cute little thing. She seems to be breathing all right now. The gagging's stopped?"

"Yes, but—"

"Dog's name?" The woman sat back down. Pen in hand, she waited for Bernadette's response.

"Mopsy. She's my sister's dog. I'm dog-sitting."

"Age?"

"Age?" Bern wasn't sure how old Mopsy was. Was it four years ago Effie had written that she'd gotten a new puppy? Five?

The sound of the outside door opening behind her broke her concentration. Bern glanced that way and watched a German shepherd limp into the office, its tan and charcoal gray coat covered with mud. The man behind the dog was just as dirty, with mud clinging to his boots and soaked into his ragged jeans. Even his worn leather jacket, partially unzipped to show a dingy white T-shirt, was spattered with mud.

He didn't seem to notice that his dog had stopped in front of him, not until he nearly ran into the animal. Sidestepping to avoid a collision, he bumped into one of the chairs, making a clatter and nearly knocking the chair over. He caught it quickly, righting it again, before looking her way.

An embarrassed grin switched to an unabashed stare as his gaze traveled from her sleekly pulled-back blond hair, over her charcoal gray wool coat, to the toes of her black pumps. For a moment Bernadette could imagine how a model felt on the runway, both her body and outfit being closely examined. When his eyes met hers, the grin returned, clearly sexual, and she knew she'd passed his scrutiny. Not that she was surprised. Most men found her attractive, at least initially.

Her reaction to him wasn't as positive. Dirt, in her opinion, wasn't attractive, and she'd never seen anyone so dirty, at least not since first grade, when Billy Doster was showing off and fell headfirst into a mud puddle. Unlike Billy, this guy was not only dirty, he needed a shave and a haircut.

She supposed, if you took away the dirt, he could be called good-looking. Actually, if he had that shave and a shower, and about three inches taken off his mop of brown hair, she might call him handsome. He certainly had the body. Broad shoulders. Narrow waist. No beer gut. For a man in his mid-thirties, which was her guess, he looked darn good.

He walked toward her, the grin widening as he neared, and Bernadette realized she'd been staring. The guy thought she was interested. Which, of course, couldn't be further from the truth, though the accelerated beat of her heart was disturbing—very disturbing—and she couldn't seem to draw her gaze away from his face.

Only when he was standing beside her did he turn his attention to the receptionist. "Here we are again, Joy. Doc in?"

"He's finishing a spaying." Joy, the receptionist,

Destiny Unknown

again rose to her feet and looked over the side of the counter. "What happened to you this time, Thor?"

The dog wagged his tail at the sound of his name, and the man patted him on his head. "He decided it was easier to go through a window than a door. Problem was, the window wasn't open. He's got a pretty nasty cut on his leg. Looks like it's going to take some stitches."

"We'll get you right in."

"Hey!" Bern snapped out of her stupor. "Right in" had had the sound of "before anyone else."

Both Joy and Mr. Sex Appeal looked at her, and Bern lifted Mopsy slightly, so they could see. "I have a sick dog here. A very sick dog. And I have to get back to work."

Joy grinned. "You're going to love this, Cody. *Her* dog ate a sponge."

Cody chuckled, the sound fittingly deep and rumbly. Bernadette frowned. "I don't think it's funny. She was choking."

Immediately his smile vanished. "Sorry. I wasn't laughing at that. It's just that it sounds so familiar. When Thor was a pup, he made a valiant attempt to eat a dish towel. You tried oil?"

"Oil?"

"Mineral oil. Fish oil. Most any kind will work. Helps grease the skids, so to speak."

She got the picture. To her dismay, she was getting several pictures. Looking into his eyes was like looking into a box of Godiva chocolates, the rich brown coloring so tempting. Looking at his hair, she realized three small gold hoop earrings adorned his left ear.

He seemed to have a preference for gold jewelry. Besides the earrings, he wore a gold chain around his neck. Curious, she checked his left hand.

No gold ring.

Not that his marital status mattered . . . or even his sexual preferences. She wasn't interested. She liked men who wore suits—Armani suits preferred—who kept their hair cut short, and who overall had a successful demeanor. With this guy, not only was the Armani suit missing, his jeans were torn at the knees.

"How long ago did your dog eat this sponge?" he asked, and she realized her gaze had dropped to his jeans, and it wasn't his knees that she'd been concentrating on.

"How long ago?" Shifting Mopsy so that she was cradling the dog in front of her, Bernadette glanced at her watch. "I'm not exactly sure. I'd left her in my office while I was checking on those sponges." She made a guess. "Maybe half an hour ago. Forty, forty-five minutes at most."

Cody reached forward. Bern tensed and stepped back.

"I want to see how distended her belly is," he said, the lift of his bushy brown eyebrows questioning her retreat.

"Don't be afraid. He really knows dogs," Joy said.

"I'm not afraid." Bernadette stepped forward again, letting Cody touch Mopsy's belly. "You'll find it hard as a rock."

Gently he pressed on the dog's sides. His hands were covered with nicks and cuts, and dirt was ground under his nails and into his knuckles. They were callused hands. Hands that did manual labor. Definitely not the hands of a successful businessman.

He poked and he prodded, yet Mopsy wasn't distressed by his handling. If anything, the dog seemed to relax.

Destiny Unknown
13

Bernadette couldn't say the same, not with him standing so close. The tension vibrating through her was unnerving, her senses in overdrive. She could smell the leather of his jacket and the sweat of his body, could hear the rhythm of his breathing and the soft hum of the words he used to soothe Mopsy. Intrigued, she listened; the sound of his voice was mesmerizing.

Then she felt his fingertips rub against her coat, putting pressure on her breasts, and the spark of awareness that shot through her fired her imagination. She pulled back, her body tingling, but he'd already moved his hand and had turned away. Seemingly unaware of what he'd done, he spoke to Joy. "Better tell Jim to put on his raincoat. Unless I miss my guess, he's got a repeat performance coming up."

Joy laughed and left her desk. "I'll tell him. In fact, I think I'll go see how he's doing."

Alone with Cody in the waiting room, Bern fought back a sense of uneasiness. He smiled at her. She looked away.

"Shih tzu?" he asked.

"She what?" Bernadette looked back, frowning.

"Is she a shih tzu? It's a breed of dog."

"I know what it is." She simply hadn't been thinking about the dog, not with him so near. "She's only part."

"Have you had her long?"

"Less than twenty-four hours." She liked the fact that her answer took him aback. "She belongs to my sister. I'm just dog-sitting while she's on her honeymoon."

He nodded and patted his own dog's head. "They do pick the most inopportune times to get into trouble."

"If you say so. I wouldn't know. I've never owned a

dog." She wrinkled her nose. "Personally, I find them smelly and messy."

"You sound like my mother."

From his tone, Bernadette knew that wasn't a compliment.

"Do you have any kids?" he asked.

The question surprised her. "No, I'm not married."

He nodded. "That's good."

No explanation. Simply a statement. She didn't understand. "Meaning?"

"Nothing in particular, other than that I hate seeing families where the kids want a dog, but the parents won't let them because dogs are smelly and messy." He imitated her wrinkling her nose. "For some of us a dog is like part of the family."

Bernadette glanced down at his dog and the mud caked on the animal's coat, then at Cody and the mud caked on his jeans and jacket. "I do see a family resemblance."

"Both good-looking, right?" He patted his dog's head, and Thor wagged his tail.

"If you say so." Turning away, Bernadette walked over to the plastic chairs lining the wall. She needed distance between them, some way to escape the tension radiating through her.

Cody watched her sit down. She turned her head so that she was looking away from him, the gesture a clear snub. From the moment he'd stepped through the door, she'd been wrinkling her pretty little nose at him. Her attitude was regal, her opinion clear. She'd judged, and he'd failed.

Why, then, didn't he leave it at that? Accept that once again he was being judged by appearances? Every logical brain cell he possessed told him to forget her. It

Destiny Unknown

wasn't as though he needed to make a conquest. Attracting women had never been a problem for him. And he certainly didn't need to subjugate himself to verbal abuse. He'd had enough of that growing up.

So why did he stroll across the room, Thor by his side, and sit down beside Ms. Ice Princess?

He supposed he could blame his actions on a perverse sense of humor. It was funny, watching her stiffen her back and edge away, all the while maintaining a tightly controlled smile and avoiding eye contact. Knowing she wanted to tell him to get lost, yet didn't, amused him. For most of his childhood he'd been called dumb. It had bothered him then, when he couldn't escape the barbed tongues and couldn't fight back. Now he'd learned that playing dumb could be fun. The fool became the mocker.

"Name's Cody," he said, holding out his hand. "William Cody Taylor actually, but everyone calls me Cody."

She looked at his outstretched hand, but didn't move.

"And yours is?" He pushed, waiting.

She still didn't offer her hand, but she did give her name. "Bernadette Sanders."

Immediately she looked away. He kept at it. "Oh, and let me introduce my son—Thor."

She glanced down at his dog, then back at him, a frown flickering across her face. Cody let his gaze travel from her blond hair—not one strand of which was out of place—to a face that was expertly made up, to a coat that probably cost more than most people made in a month. "So you're not married," he said aloud. "That means you're either single or divorced. Let me see . . ." He rubbed his chin and remembered he hadn't shaved. It had been a heck of a morning. "My guess is you're a—" He made a wild guess. "Stockbroker?"

She gave a slight shake of her head. Irritated. Dismissive.

"No?" He searched for other professions where outward appearances were important. "Realtor?" He was familiar with most of the realtors around Grand Rapids, but she could be new.

Her no to that suggestion was terse and barely audible. He was bothering her, all right. He kept at it. "Boy, I'm not doing well at this, am I? Doctor? Lawyer?" He chuckled. "Indian chief?"

Her glance would have cooled ice. "If you must know, I'm the general manager of Morgan's Department Stores."

She pronounced her answer as a final statement. He wasn't about to let up, though. "Oh yeah? Which one? The downtown store or the one on Twenty-eighth Street?"

"Both."

He was impressed. Not that he would let her know. "Well, heck, if you're managing Parker's stores, that practically makes us fellow employees. I did some work for him a few years back."

The nose went up again. "You worked at one of his stores?"

He played to her expectations. "No. This was construction work. I hammered a few nails here and there for the guy."

"I see." Once again she looked him over.

He knew she didn't see. She was blinded by the externals.

Her gaze went to the doorway Joy had disappeared through. "I wonder what's taking her so long?"

"Jim probably asked her to give him a hand." Cody reached over and touched the little dog on her lap.

Bernadette's gaze snapped to his face. "What are you doing?"

"Just feeling her stomach. Seeing if there's been any change."

"And?" She watched his hand, her body tense.

He combed his fingers into the dog's long hair. Though her belly was distended, it wasn't a life-threatening situation. A good physic was all the dog needed. "Feels about the same."

"When I found her gagging . . ." For a moment the haughtiness slipped, concern softening Bernadette's eyes to a velvety shade of blue. "If anything should happen to her . . ."

She took in a deep breath, and the rigid control was put back in place. She might say she didn't like dogs, Cody thought, but she cared about this one.

He didn't want to feel sorry for her. Feeling sorry for a woman had gotten him into trouble once. And he didn't want to be attracted to her. She reminded him too much of the people who had ridiculed him when he was growing up.

Angry with himself, Cody dug his fingers into the ruff around his dog's neck. "How you doing, boy?"

Thor thumped his tail on the floor in response and lay his head on Cody's knee with an almost human sigh. Cody sensed that Bernadette was watching. He played her game and ignored her. Carefully he lifted Thor's leg, checking for signs of new bleeding. He would take second place to a gluttonous moppet only as long as his dog's life wasn't in danger.

There was no fresh bleeding.

"Is that . . ." Bernadette hesitated, and he glanced

her way. Nose wrinkled, she pointed at the underpants he'd wrapped around Thor's leg.

He grinned, knowing someone like her would never use old underwear for rags or bandages. "Figured it was better than using these jeans." He slapped his thigh, giving the impression that he was wearing nothing under the denims. "Could you check and see if you think I've wrapped his leg too tight?"

She didn't move. Not that he expected her to. She saw him as the fool, all right, just as his stepfather and stepbrothers had.

Chuckling, Cody let Thor rest his paw on the floor again. "I guess you don't need to. I always buy briefs with plenty of stretch. You know, just in case."

She said nothing, and he leaned toward her, letting the sleeve of his jacket brush against the sleeve of her coat. He heard her intake of breath, and he struggled not to laugh.

If she'd looked, she would have seen that the sleeve was clean. Then again, maybe she thought he had cooties. "You been Parker's general manager for long?" he asked.

"Seven months." She leaned a little away from him.

"And before that?"

"I managed a store in Chicago." Every word was tightly spoken.

"So, what brought you to Grand Rapids?"

Bernadette glared at him as Cody sat back in his chair, looking totally relaxed. She didn't want to talk to him, much less tell him her reasons for moving to Grand Rapids. She gave the answer that satisfied most people. The easiest answer. "I grew up not far from here. Coming back to Grand Rapids was like coming home."

"And not far from here is—?"

"Gun Lake."

"I see. And are you now commuting from Gun Lake?"

"No, I've got an apartment here in town."

"Which one?"

He was sneaky, she'd give him that. He was also totally dense. Most men would have gotten her message by now. With this one it was obvious she'd have to be more direct. "Mr. . . . ah—"

"Taylor," he supplied, sitting straighter in his chair.

"Mr. Taylor, I appreciate your assistance with Mopsy, but I'm not interested in anything else you might have to offer." Not even his hammer. Maybe Parker had used him for some work, but she wouldn't be hiring him for the remodeling. Not with his attitude. "I—"

He didn't let her finish. "How do you know you're not interested? You don't even know me."

"And I'm not going to get to know you."

"I'm a fascinating guy."

She laughed. She couldn't help it. Here he looked like he'd just ridden into town on his Harley, and he was acting like she should be panting all over him. "I think 'egotistical' better describes you."

"I've been called worse."

"I can imagine."

"What would you call me?"

She glanced down at his jeans. "Dirty."

He shrugged nonchalantly. "It's a February thaw. Ground's turned to mud."

"So what did you do, go out and roll in it?"

"I was looking at an old house. Thor went through that window and cut his leg. Tending to him, I got dirty.

For some reason, I thought getting Thor here was more important than taking a shower and changing."

Perhaps he had a point. Still . . .

"It's more than just the dirt, isn't it?"

She said nothing.

"What? The long hair? The holes in my jeans? Or is it the earrings?" He touched a finger to the gold hoops. "Do we have a few prejudices there?"

"*We?* I don't know about you, but I don't have any prejudices. Your sexual preferences and how you choose to dress are your business."

"I'm glad to hear that. Not that you had to worry. I can assure you my sexual preferences are for women, and only for women."

"How nice, I'm sure." His assumption that she would even care was ridiculous.

"I will confess I'm a klutz. Me and my dog. Or is it my dog and I?"

"Whatever." She simply wished he'd leave her alone. Go away. Stop talking. Do something. He made her uneasy.

"Must be my clothes," he said nonchalantly. "Haven't you heard, clothes don't make the man?"

Bernadette couldn't let that pass. "You're saying that to someone in the clothing business. And I disagree. Clothes can make the man . . . or woman. How a person looks is very important. To *be* successful, you must *look* successful."

"And make lots of money?" He grinned. "If I were rich, would you be interested in me then? Would you go out with me?"

He was making her sound like a gold digger. "Money isn't important to me."

"Good. Have lunch with me."

Destiny Unknown

"Lunch?" His invitation stunned her.

"Yeah." He smiled, then frowned. "No. Lunch might be difficult considering the shape these two dogs are in. Let's make it dinner. Tonight. You choose the restaurant. I'll even shower and change to a new pair of jeans."

She laughed again. He was incorrigible. "I don't think I'm getting through to you. Let me say this as clearly as I can. I am not interested in going out with you. Not to lunch or to dinner. We're sharing space in a veterinarian's office. That's all."

"You've got a nice laugh, you know?" His grin carried to his eyes. "And you're wrong. We're doing more than sharing space. There's an attraction. Probably shouldn't be, but—"

She couldn't let him go on. "Mr. Taylor, you are the last man on earth I'd be attracted to. You and I are—are . . ."

She couldn't think of the word to describe what they were, and was glad when Joy stepped back into the reception area. "The doctor will see you now," she said to Bernadette.

TWO

"Mopsy, please." Bernadette crawled toward the corner of the kitchen where the dog had taken refuge. Bernadette was not only tearing and scattering the newspapers she'd spread over the linoleum, she was getting the print all over the knees of her winter-white wool slacks. In one hand she clutched a teaspoon and the bottle of mineral oil that the veterinarian had given her. Her other hand was free and poised.

In the last hour Mopsy had become quite adept at avoiding her. She was one quick dog. Bernadette was almost close enough to make a grab for the dog, but she knew what would happen when she did. Like a flash, Mopsy would dart past her and into another corner, and the coaxing would start all over again.

"Please, Mopsy," Bernadette cajoled. Warily the dog watched her. Bernadette inched closer, held her breath, and grabbed.

Her doorbell rang the same moment the dog streaked past her. Swearing, Bernadette sat back on her heels. This was ridiculous. Effie would be back from her

Destiny Unknown

honeymoon before she had that damned teaspoon of oil in Mopsy.

Exasperated, she released a sigh and pushed her hair back from her face. Her day at the stores had been bad enough. She didn't need this.

Again the doorbell rang.

"I'm coming, I'm coming," she yelled, and pushed herself to her feet. She wasn't expecting anyone. The few friends she'd made in the last seven months weren't the type to just drop by.

As she was leaving the kitchen she made certain the dog didn't escape and shut the door firmly. Considering how often Mopsy had used those newspapers since being shut in there, Bernadette wasn't sure why the dog needed more oil. It certainly wouldn't do to have Mopsy running loose in an apartment with white carpeting.

"Who's there?" she called through the front door, using the peephole as well.

"Cody. Cody Taylor. We met in the vet's office this morning. Remember?"

She remembered. How could she forget? All afternoon, images of him had popped into her mind. After she'd left the veterinarian's office and dropped Mopsy off at her apartment, Bernadette had walked by a display of gold earrings and chains in the store's jewelry department and had thought of Cody Taylor. Then, when she was in Housewares and Gifts, the chocolates they sold had reminded her of his eyes. Even a rack of jeans in the men's department had triggered an unbidden memory.

She didn't open the door. "If this is about dinner, I said no."

"Everyone's entitled to a mistake, but that's not why I'm here. I have something for you."

"What?" She was wary of men bearing gifts.

"Two books. One from the vet's office and one I had. You might find them helpful."

Considering her futile attempts in the last hour to medicate Mopsy, she could use some help. Not that she thought letting Cody into her apartment was wise or that two books were the answer. Desperation, however, overruled wisdom. With the flipping of one knob and the turning of another, she released the deadbolt and opened the door. "Enter."

Cody stared at the woman standing in front of him. The voice and the eyes were the same—the former cool and businesslike, the latter a startling blue—but what he saw stunned him. No longer pulled back, her hair flowed down past her shoulders, each strand a shade of pale gold. Gone were the tailored gray overcoat that had concealed her figure and the black pumps that had clicked her irritation when she'd last walked away from him. Her feet were now encased in creamy white slippers that looked as soft as melted butter, and the slacks and blouse she wore sweetly defined a womanly figure that could be defined as somewhere between modellike and curvaceous.

Overall, she had a softer appearance this evening, but that wasn't what kept him staring at her face. It wasn't even the smudge of black on her right cheek. What held his gaze was the line of green that ran across Bernadette's forehead.

In front of him was his enchanted princess.

Only, of course, he knew she wasn't. The mark on her forehead was merely a smudge of something green. Her skin wasn't really turning green. She wasn't under a spell. Spells and princesses were only in fairy tales, the stories his sister had told him. Fanciful tales meant to take away the sting of humiliation. Stories his sister should have listened to herself.

Cody shook his head and looked away, down toward Bernadette's knees. Only one line of green and a spot of black marred her face, whereas there were dark smudges around the knees of her slacks, as well as grease spots. The bottle of mineral oil she held in one hand gave him a clue to the grease spots, and he knew what newsprint could do to anything light colored. He hoped the green could be explained away as easily.

In a way, considering how meticulous her appearance had been earlier that day, it pleased him to see a little dirt on her now. At least she was acquainted with the substance. As one who knew it well, he'd felt it best to shower, shave, and change before coming by her place. Not that he wanted to impress her. Nor had he changed all that much. He'd merely replaced the boots with loafers, and the holey jeans with a newer, far less threadbare pair. The jacket was the same. Winter, spring, and fall, it was his standby. All he'd done was clean off the mud, which it had needed, anyhow. And he had slipped on one of his nicer polo shirts. But not to impress her.

He was here for a purpose, and one purpose only. To offer help. He held the two books toward her. "One has some first aid tips. Jim sent it. The other, I've had around for years. It has some pretty good information on dogs."

She took the books, but didn't look at them. "And will they tell me how to catch a dog that doesn't want to be caught, how to get her mouth open without spilling the spoonful of oil, and how to hold on to her once she decides I'm seriously going to try to pour the stuff in her mouth?"

Frustration laced her words. He knew the feeling. "Things not going well?"

She shook her head, a wave of golden hair sliding over her silk blouse with a whisper. "If I ever wondered why I didn't want a dog, Mopsy is convincing me."

"Jim said you were nervous about all this." Cody grinned. "He also said you nearly passed out while you were in his office."

She wrinkled her nose. "I've always said dogs were messy and smelly, but I had no idea things would get that messy . . . and smelly."

"What goes in must come out. I remember how it was the time Thor ate the dish towel." He grinned. "Would you like some help?"

"Yes." There was no hesitation. She started for a closed door inside her apartment, and he followed, shutting the outside door behind him.

Her apartment was spacious and elegantly decorated. Neutral colors accented by touches of warmth. Nothing out of place. It was exactly what he'd expected. Ms. Sanders lived in the right neighborhood, had good taste in decor and clothes, and undoubtedly chose her friends with the same care.

He'd grown up with people like her.

She opened the kitchen door, and he saw a new image, one of chaos. He also saw her dog. Amid the torn newspapers scattered over the linoleum, the mop of long hair that had lain limply in her arms earlier that day was now very much alert and eyeing the doorway as a means of escape.

"No!" Bern yelled as Mopsy made her break for freedom.

Cody caught the streaking dog before she had a chance to dash past his legs. Scooping her up, he drew

Destiny Unknown

her close to his body. For a moment she squirmed, then he felt her relax in his arms.

Stroking the dog's head, he talked to her, but he was aware of Bernadette. She had faced him and was watching. Without changing the soothing tone of his voice or the strokes of his hand, he stepped into the kitchen. "Better close the door."

"Of course." She pushed it shut. "That was a pretty nifty move. She's been evading me since she realized what I was going to do."

"I've got a lot of nifty moves."

Bernadette arched an eyebrow and allowed him a smile. "I'll bet you do."

She led the way to the kitchen table, and he followed. Much as he hated to admit it, Bernadette Sanders had some "nifty moves" too. There was an elegance to her posture and a grace to her steps. Her height helped, he was sure, and considering the top of her head came to his chin, he guessed she was around five feet seven or eight. But it was more than her height; it was an attitude. The lady had class.

How badly his sister had wanted that.

At the table, Bernadette set down the bottle of oil, the teaspoon, and the two books he'd given her. He chose the nearest chair and sat, making certain his hold on Mopsy was secure. No sense in spoiling his hero image by getting lax. "How much of that oil is she supposed to have?"

Bernadette glanced at the bottle. "Just a teaspoonful tonight. The vet said that should finish the job. And if not, a teaspoon in the morning would."

Cody had already felt the dog's stomach and knew it was relaxed. The odor lingering in the kitchen and the papers on the floor indicated the laxative Jim had given the dog had done the necessary job. One more teaspoon would be all that was needed. "You spoon; I'll hold," he said, and cradled Mopsy in his arms like a quarterback hugging a football.

"You want me to do it?" She hesitated, then shrugged and opened the bottle. Carefully she filled the spoon, then stepped toward him.

He spread his legs, inviting her to come closer. To his surprise, she did, her gaze alternately on the dog and the spoon in her hand. She was so intent on getting the oil into Mopsy, he doubted she even noticed when her thighs touched his. He was aware of the contact, however. Too aware, he decided as his body immediately reacted. He was also aware of the delightful smell of her body and the way her breasts pressed against the silk of her blouse. If he leaned forward, he could touch one with his lips.

He resisted the urge and focused his attention on the dog. Using the pressure of his fingers at the back of Mopsy's jaw, he opened her mouth. The oil was poured in, and he quickly closed Mopsy's mouth, holding it closed until he felt the little dog swallow. Then he began stroking her again, telling her what a good girl she was.

"That was easy." Bernadette stepped back, afraid her voice might have sounded a little shaky. Maybe Cody hadn't noticed, but his legs had practically encompassed hers. For a moment their bodies had actually touched. Had she known him better, she would have called the position intimate.

Who was she kidding? Considering the way her skin was still tingling, the contact had been intimate. Being that close to him had all of her shaking, not just her voice. She could tell herself she didn't find men with

Destiny Unknown

earrings and long hair appealing, but this one was turning her into a liar.

She pulled out a chair and sat. "Slam, bam, thank you, ma'am."

His eyebrows rose, and she realized what she'd said. "I mean, that certainly didn't take long."

He simply smiled, and she tried again. "That is—"

"You're blushing."

"I am not." But the heat in her face belied that. "I just—" She fought for control. "I was merely surprised. I thought that was going to be a struggle. Instead, it was over before I realized. How can I thank you?"

His smile was suggestive.

"Other than that way."

Chuckling, Cody glanced around her kitchen. "You could offer me a drink."

A drink sounded good to her. A glass of white wine maybe. "What would you like? I don't have any beer, but I do have some wine, and . . ." She tried to remember what else. "Oh yes, a little vodka."

His gaze came back to her face, a slight frown drawing his dark brows together. "Do you have any tea?"

"Tea?" It wasn't what she'd expected. "Iced or hot?"

"Hot." He smiled and scratched Mopsy behind the ears. "We lived with my grandmother when I was little, before my mother remarried. Every evening she'd have a cup of hot tea. 'English tea,' she called it. And if I was good, I could join her. Of course, mine was mostly milk and sugar."

"I have some English tea."

He grinned. "I still take it with milk and sugar."

If she was making one cup of tea, she might as well make two. Forget the wine. And for English tea it seemed appropriate to heat up the teakettle on the stove instead of sticking a mug of water in the microwave, as she usually did. "How is your dog doing?" she asked as she brought the sugar bowl down from the cupboard.

"He's fine, thank you. He's traded in my briefs for seven stitches and an adhesive bandage."

From the refrigerator she got the milk. When she turned and faced him again, the reality of his being in her kitchen hit her. There was a question she hadn't asked, she realized. "How did you know where I lived?"

"Would you believe I followed a path through the enchanted woods and it led me to your doorstep?"

"No." But she would believe that Joy the receptionist had given him her address. "Don't you ever give up?"

"Not when there's a princess to be rescued."

She wasn't sure about the princess part, but she'd needed his help this evening. "This has been a heck of a day. One thing after another. I don't feel like I've accomplished anything, even tonight. I was going to give myself a facial, but Miss Mopsy started raising a fuss. I was afraid she was going to disturb the neighbors."

His smile was enigmatic, his gaze on her face. "When you give yourself a facial, what do you do?"

It wasn't a question men usually asked. Oh, Loren McVeigh, the art director at Morgan's, might, but talking to Loren was sometimes like talking to another woman. Perhaps Cody Taylor wasn't as much a "man" as her body was telling her. "I give myself a facial sauna, then use a masque for deep cleaning, followed by a toner and a moisturizer. Why?"

"Just curious. And do these masques come in colors? Like maybe green?"

"Green?" Bernadette frowned, truly confused. "Yes. In fact, the one I have is green. Why?"

His eyes turned into smooth cocoa with his grin.

Destiny Unknown

31

"It's a long story. I—" He placed a hand on Mopsy's belly, then quickly set the dog on one of the newspapers on the floor.

As soon as Mopsy had relieved herself he wrapped up the papers. "Is there somewhere—?"

Bern gave him directions to the Dumpster out back. The moment he left the kitchen, she leaned back against the counter, her legs shaking and her heart racing. Cody Taylor wasn't like Loren McVeigh. What he resembled was a tornado. From the moment he'd stepped into the veterinarian's office that morning, he'd had her thoughts and emotions in a whirl. She didn't want to find him attractive, but she did. Didn't want to be around him, but here he was, in her apartment, and she'd actually been glad to see him.

Because you needed help, she told herself. That's all.

So what if her body had reacted when his legs touched hers? All that proved was that she was human. The demands of her job might have kept her from having time for men; that didn't mean her body was dead. A year without a date was too long. "You need to get out more." She got down two teacups. "Need to find a man."

A man who fit into her lifestyle. A man who would stick around.

It wouldn't be someone like Cody Taylor.

She laughed at the idea of her being attracted to Cody. Her sister was always telling her she had to stop finding fault with every man she dated. Well, she hadn't even known Cody twenty-four hours, and she'd found lots to fault. His clothes. His hair. His brazen attitude.

No, Cody would get his cup of tea, a little conversation, and then he was out of her life. This wouldn't even be a case of her leaving him before he left her. There would be no getting together at all. The ministering of one teaspoon of oil and a trip to the Dumpster did not change anything. He might be persistent, but she wasn't going out with him.

When Cody returned, the tea was steeping in a pot on the table, with two cups, a creamer, and sugar bowl beside it. A spraying of room freshener had eliminated most of the odor, and Bernadette had laid down more newspapers, covering the linoleum neatly once again. On the counter by the sink she'd set a towel. She motioned toward it. "You can wash up."

He took off his jacket, draping it over the back of his chair. Bernadette noted the polo shirt he was wearing was quality merchandise, the fit perfect. It was a giant step up from what he'd been wearing that morning. His best, she guessed.

He turned to the sink and pumped soap into his palms, and she found herself staring at his back. She admired men who were cultured and sophisticated, yet simply watching Cody's back muscles stretch and contract as he scrubbed his hands had her pulse racing. There was a clean definition to his shoulders and biceps that suggested strength developed from hard labor rather than long hours in an exercise gym. There was also an earthiness about him that she was sure no amount of soap would wash away.

Watching the play of his muscles evoked memories of how his thighs had felt against her legs. Unsuitable or not, he had a body to die for, and she couldn't stop herself from wondering how he would look without any clothes on.

"Want to see?" he asked.

Destiny Unknown

33

She sucked in a breath, afraid he'd read her mind.

Turning toward her, he held up his hands. "Almost clean."

Relief rippled through her in a laugh. "What do you want, a gold star?"

"Of course." He grabbed the towel on the counter.

"Sorry, all out of gold stars." Her gaze went to the gold chain around his neck, then to the gold earrings. "You like gold, don't you?"

He touched the chain. "It has meaning."

"Such as?"

He looked at her forehead and grinned. "I'll tell you sometime."

He tossed the towel onto the counter. It slipped off and onto the papers covering the floor. Picking it up again, he chuckled. "I'm certainly playing out my part of the story. The clumsy oaf, always dropping things and tripping over his own two feet. The daydreamer. How do you feel about klutzes?"

"I wouldn't want you working in Glassware. But then, I also hate seeing mothers with young children go into that department."

Cody walked toward the table. "No dogs. No children. You said you're not married. Have you ever been married?"

"No." She sat straighter in her chair as he neared. Why his being close made her edgy, she didn't know. She wasn't afraid of him, and she wasn't normally edgy around any man. "It's not that I dislike dogs." She didn't feel she owed him an explanation, but talking helped ease the tension. "And I don't dislike children. They just"—she glanced down at the newspapers covering her kitchen floor—"cause problems."

"Women also cause problems. Having been married for five years, I can attest to that."

"You're married?" The way he'd looked at her earlier wasn't the way a married man should have looked at her.

"Past tense," he said, and again took the chair opposite her. "I mistook Bev's green hair as a sign, thought I was supposed to help her."

"You're saying your wife had green hair?"

"It was green the day I met her. Something about the chlorine in the swimming pool and the bleach she'd used on her hair. It happened twice more while we were married." He shook his head. "She made a lot of mistakes over and over. She was an alcoholic, and her going off the wagon was a repeat performance I finally couldn't handle anymore. Maybe we never learn. She's married again, still drinking—as far as I know—and I'm still a sucker for a woman with a problem."

Bernadette hoped he didn't see her as a woman with a problem. "I'm quite capable of solving my own problems."

"I'm sure you are." His grin said otherwise. "Of course, that's not how it looked when I first got here tonight."

"I'd hardly consider getting a teaspoon of oil down a dog a major problem." Certainly not compared to other things that had gone wrong that day.

Cody looked at Mopsy, not her. "What do you think, puppy dog? Were you a major problem?"

The moment he acknowledged Mopsy's presence, she barked and began dancing around on her hind legs. His expression registered his surprise. "That's quite a trick."

"Actually, Mopsy's quite well trained," Bernadette

said. Not that she knew the commands for the tricks. "My sister uses her in a clown act. That's Mopsy's way of asking for attention."

"So, we're still friends?" He scooped up Mopsy, once again cradling the dog in his arms. Crooning to her, he scratched her belly.

Bernadette sipped her tea, listening to Cody talk to the dog. He was a strange man. Rugged looking, yet gentle acting. He definitely had a way with animals. Even she found his voice soothing. Mesmerizing.

"You're good with dogs." And women, she was sure. "You said you were married for five years. Any children?"

"No." He grinned her way. "Just my son, Thor, who gets into enough trouble."

"I'll tell you one thing," she said. "I'm not leaving any more sponges around Mopsy."

Cody nodded his agreement. "Since Thor ate part of that dish towel, I'm very careful whenever I wipe up spilled meat juices. Either I rinse everything out, or I put it where he can't get to it."

"That's what's odd." It had bothered her all afternoon. "I'm sure that when I left my office, I pushed my chair up to the desk so Mopsy couldn't get to the soup. The only thing I can surmise is that when Ben went back for the purchase order, he moved the chair."

"Ben?"

"He's our resource manager at Morgan's. Besides suggesting ways to save or make money, he's great with customer complaints. We had some about a batch of sponges that wouldn't absorb liquids. That's what started all this."

"Nonabsorbent sponges aren't good."

"Not good at all, but par for the day. Seems like now that the boss is away, everything's going wrong. Since eight o'clock this morning it's been one thing after another. Downtown, one of our EAS—electronic article surveillance—systems started going off this afternoon. Sometimes a cellular phone will set them off, but we couldn't find any reason for this. It would just go off, then start working fine, then go off again. It was crazy. And if that wasn't enough, Consumers Power shut the electricity off at the Twenty-eighth Street store for over ten minutes, and three deliveries were completely messed up for both stores. Days like this make me wonder why I'm in the business."

"So, why are you?"

She smiled. "The money's good."

"Money isn't everything."

A typical response for those who didn't have any. She had her own pat response. "Beats worrying about how to pay the bills."

"Is that a cliché or spoken from experience?"

Bernadette shrugged. "I can't say money's ever been a big worry in my life, but I saw how it was with the people who came to Gun Lake who had lots of money. It didn't take me long to decide I'd rather be rich than just getting by."

"And how much are you willing to sacrifice to be rich?"

A lift of her eyebrows expressed her surprise at the question. "If you're asking would I do anything illegal, the answer is no."

"Sacrificing your principles doesn't have to be illegal. When a person has to fit a mold to succeed, the price is too high."

"Some molds have a purpose. They let a person know what to expect."

"I remember one of my college professors telling me he never knew what to expect from me. He meant it as a put-down. I took it as a compliment."

"You went to college?" That surprised her. Or maybe it shouldn't have. She really didn't know him at all.

"Went and dropped out."

She nodded, and Cody could imagine what she was thinking. He could tell her more, but decided against it. Let her make her assumptions, right or wrong. Lifting his hand from Mopsy's head, he reached for the creamer. "What about you, Bernadette Sanders? Do you have a college degree and all that?"

"I graduated from Western Michigan University with a major in business administration. Summa cum laude."

"Summa cum laude. I'm impressed. And let me guess. You started out managing a small store, moved on to a bigger store, then bigger." He cocked her a smile. "And in the end, where will you be?"

"Here, if I do well. Parker wants to step aside, take only a peripheral position in the management. A year or two from now, I could be CEO and Director of Stores. Not bad for a woman in her early thirties."

"Not bad at all," he agreed. "But what do you do if that perfect man does come along?"

Her smile was wry. I don't think I need to worry about that."

"You never know."

"Let's put it this way, it would be a surprise to me."

"Life is full of surprises." Such as finding a woman with green on her face, he mused, a woman who aroused him. Leaning back in his chair, he grinned. "So, Ms. Sanders, when are we going out to dinner?"

"Now, *that* would be a surprise." She laughed and shook her head. "I hope you don't think an invitation into my apartment meant I'd changed my mind about you. We . . . that is— Well, let's just say I'm not interested in pursuing this any further than a thank-you for your help."

"Big mistake. I'm one of a kind."

"You think so?"

"Ever met anyone else like me?"

"Dozens. And I found them all bores. They call themselves the X generation. The dropouts marching to their own drummer."

"Ah, but I'm different from them."

"You have a steady job? Go to work every day?"

He grinned. "I'm working on a new project."

"Right."

"I keep busy."

"Sure." She smiled knowingly, then shrugged. "Look, maybe I can help. We're going to make some changes at Morgan's. Move a couple of departments closer, redesign their layouts and change the color scheme. If you'd be interested . . ."

She was throwing him a crumb. "You offering me this so we can be near each other?"

"No." That idea clearly startled her. "I'm offering you the job so you can earn some money."

He shook his head. "Naw, I don't think so."

"In other words, you're happy living as you are?" She made the idea sound pathetic.

"I march to my own drummer, remember?" Setting Mopsy down, he pushed back his chair. "I suppose, if you don't want me around, I'd better be going."

Destiny Unknown

"Well, it is getting late." She also stood, all prim and proper. "I do want to thank you for your assistance with Mopsy. I'll read those books, then return them to the veterinarian. I'm sure he'll get your books back to you."

"I'm sure he will." The ice princess was making it clear she didn't want to see him again. Not that she would. After tonight he would be out of her life.

But first he wanted to apply some heat, melt a little of the ice.

Grinning, Cody walked around the table until he was directly in front of her. "You're turning green, my dear, and I don't think it's with envy." He ran a fingertip over the line of dried clay and chemicals on her forehead, and bits of green flaked off.

"What the—?" She stared at the traces of the masque that clung to his finger.

"Farewell, Princess." Tilting her head back, he kissed her.

She hadn't expected him to kiss her, so she didn't stop him. And it didn't start out as a passionate kiss. Actually, all he had meant to do was irritate her.

And why not? It irritated him that she'd judged him on his appearance. Irritated him that he found her attractive.

Oh yes, he only meant the kiss to be a teaser, certainly nothing more. But somewhere between the initial touching of their lips and a millisecond later, all those thoughts changed, and he was kissing her because he wanted to, because he enjoyed the small catch of her breath and the way her eyes widened.

Sparks of awareness flashed in those eyes, points of light in a sea of blue. Sparks were flashing through him as well. Dangerous sparks that could cause real trouble.

Jerking back, he stared at her, dumbfounded by his own stupidity. He should have known, should have suspected he was playing with fire. Before she moved, he grabbed his jacket and headed for the door. "I can let myself out," he said, and was gone.

THREE

"He doesn't understand an artistic temperament."

Loren McVeigh, all six feet of him, stood next to Bernadette, pouting like a little boy who couldn't get his way. The man opposite him was acting just as childish. Benjamin Waite had come to her office whining that Loren had changed the window displays without consulting him. Mediating arguments between the two was becoming a daily occurrence.

"This has got to stop," she said, knowing the problem was more than one man not understanding the other's "artistic" temperament. Straitlaced Ben, who attended church on a regular basis, was nearing forty, and was married with two children, also didn't understand Loren's lifestyle.

"Maybe he considers it inconsequential," Ben argued, "but we did decide to emphasize family this Easter. It was *your* idea, in fact."

"It's a bunny family," Loren said. "They're showing togetherness by holding hands."

"They're both dressed in men's clothing."

Loren raised his neatly trimmed eyebrows. "So?"

"All right, enough," Bernadette said. She'd heard this before. They were getting nowhere. "Ben, you know Loren has the freedom to change the window designs if he feels it's necessary. But, Loren, if you want bunnies, I suggest you add one more dressed as a female, and drop the hand-holding. This is Grand Rapids, not San Francisco."

"Oh fine, take his side." Loren lifted his chin. "One of these days I'll be working for a company that has stores outside of this narrow-minded community."

"Feel free to apply anytime," Ben told him.

"I said, enough!" Bernadette knew this would lead to another argument. "And in the future, Ben, take care of this yourself. You weren't hired to come running to me every five minutes."

"No, I was hired for your job." He lifted his chin as high as Loren had and marched off.

Loren gave her one more look of disdain and headed in the opposite direction.

"Some days you just can't win."

Her thoughts exactly, but Bernadette hadn't expected to hear them voiced aloud and only a few feet away. The sound of the familiar male voice sent a shiver of excitement down her spine, and she quickly turned to face Cody Taylor.

He smiled, and her stomach did a flip.

How a man so clearly opposite her tastes could have this effect on her was a puzzle. Nothing had changed. His hair was still far too long, he still wore the earrings and the gold chain, the scuffed boots and the leather jacket, and his jeans were still faded to the point of being threadbare. Although he had shaved and was undeniably good-looking, there was nothing about him that should

Destiny Unknown

have had her heart pounding or a blush rising to her cheeks.

There was no reason at all to feel light-headed.

"I was in the neighborhood and thought I'd stop by," he said.

She watched his lips move, remembering his kiss two nights ago. He'd taken her by surprise, and the kiss had been over before she'd realized what he was doing. By the time she'd snapped out of her stupor, he was out the door.

Oh, then she'd told him what she thought of him. Standing in her kitchen, her only companion Mopsy, she'd said lots of things to Cody Taylor, none of them flattering. His ears must have been burning.

She hoped they'd burned so hot he hadn't been able to sleep that night, for he'd certainly ruined her sleep. It had been embarrassing enough to look in the mirror and see the smudge of printers' ink on her cheek and the line of green across her forehead. It was all that darn dog's fault. Bernadette had remembered cleansing her face and starting with the masque. That was when Mopsy had erupted into a barking frenzy. Afraid her neighbors would complain, she'd gone to check on Mopsy and, in the kitchen, had seen the bottle of mineral oil, and had recalled she needed to give Mopsy a teaspoonful. The rest was history.

That night and since, she'd relived every word Cody had said, every look he'd given her. Over and over she'd replayed the moment his lips had touched hers. Never had such a passing kiss affected her so deeply.

"I didn't want to disturb you," he said, bringing her back to the present. "Not while you were dealing with those two."

Bernadette nodded, not sure she could speak.

"The one sounds very resentful. What happened? You take his job?"

"Basically." The word came out stronger than she'd expected, encouraging her to go on. "Before Parker hired me, Ben was the general manager. The man is great when it comes to ideas, but he's not good at making decisions. Parker didn't want to fire him, however, so when he gave me this job, he created another position for Ben, one that best uses his talents."

"Yet Ben isn't happy."

"I thought he was." Just as she'd thought she was happy, contented, and on top of the world. That was before meeting Cody. Now she wasn't so sure. To distract herself, she glanced down at his jeans. "Are you here to buy some new clothes? We're running some good sales. Or did you change your mind about that job offer?"

He grinned. "I'm here to take you to lunch."

"To lunch?" She'd thought they'd settled that. "I turned down your invitation. Remember?"

"That was Monday. It's now Wednesday, noontime, and you do need to eat."

"But not necessarily with you." Especially since seeing him had her stomach tied in knots.

He continued grinning. "Not necessarily, but ask yourself, why not?"

"Perhaps because I don't want to."

"Or perhaps because you're afraid to."

Her chin went up. "Why would I be afraid?"

"You tell me. All we're talking about is lunch. An hour at the most. Time enough for you to tell me how your dog is doing."

"I don't need an hour to tell you that. Mopsy's doing fine, thank you. Tearing up my apartment." Bernadette had decided a little loneliness was safer for the dog than bringing Mopsy back to the store. Last night, however, when she'd arrived home, she'd questioned that decision. In less than twelve hours Mopsy had unwound an entire roll of toilet paper, had emptied all of the wastebaskets, shredding every paper they contained, and had demolished Bernadette's favorite pair of slippers.

"She's probably bored," Cody said. "You can tell she's a smart little thing. Isolate her in one room and get her some toys. So why don't you want to have lunch with me? Because of my appearance?"

"Your appearance?" They'd bounced from dogs to clothes. He changed subjects as fast as her sister did.

Bernadette glanced down at his jeans, the knees worn to a pale blue. She hated to admit it, but his appearance did have something to do with her refusal.

"Afraid I'll spoil your image?" he challenged.

"This has nothing to do with my image."

"Good." He smiled. "I certainly wouldn't want to think you didn't want to be seen in the company of a working man. Especially a working man between jobs."

He'd raised his voice, and Bern cringed. People were looking. "You don't have to yell."

"Am I yelling?" He looked around, smiling at the women glancing their way. "You—" He motioned to one who was wearing a stained winter jacket, polyester slacks, and down-at-the-heels winter boots. "What do you think," he asked her, "of a store manager who doesn't appreciate people who have to live within a budget, who can't afford designer-made clothes?"

The woman looked at Bern, and Bernadette suddenly wished she wasn't wearing a Liz Claiborne suit and Gucci pumps. A customer who thought the store was out of her price range wouldn't be back. The idea was to draw in the customers, not drive them away.

"We have some very good sales going on right now," she said to the woman. "And you'll find we carry a wide variety of merchandise to fit any budget." Turning back to Cody, she said under her breath, "All right. I'll go to lunch with you. But that's it. After that, we go our separate ways and you don't bother me again."

"If that's the way you want it." He had the grin of a winner.

"That's exactly the way I want it."

Cody went with Bernadette to the office area on the second floor. Separated from the sales floor by a wall of thick bull's-eye glass blocks, the space consisted of the accounting department and management. The executive secretary's desk presided over a waiting area, holding back intruders from the president's and general manager's offices. Bernadette got her coat and boots and told the secretary where she'd be. She didn't introduce Cody.

Actually, she barely acknowledged his presence at all as they rode the escalator back down. Her stiff posture and one-word answers to his questions yelled her tension and displeasure. He knew he was pushing it again, and he wasn't sure why.

Sure, she was beautiful, but he'd walked away from a lot of beautiful women without thinking twice. And yes, the suit she was wearing was moss green, but that didn't mean she was an enchanted princess waiting for him to break some spell. There was no good reason for him to have come to the store and goaded her into having lunch with him, other than he hadn't been able to forget her since leaving her apartment.

He was pushing because she was driving him crazy.

"I thought we'd eat at one of the restaurants around here," he said, once they were out of the store. "Do you mind walking?"

"Whatever you'd like."

The icicles hanging from her words were as cold as the air surrounding them. The February thaw the previous week had been short-lived, and snow was predicted for that night. He saw her pull her coat closer and wondered if it would be better to take his truck. Then he remembered all the equipment he had piled on the front seat. It would take an hour just to clean a spot for her.

Besides, women like Bernadette Sanders didn't want to be seen riding around town in a pickup. A Cadillac or BMW better suited their image. It all came down to making the proper impression. He knew that. People on their way up drove the right cars, dined in the right restaurants.

Grinning, Cody headed for the square. He knew exactly where he would take her.

"We can't go in here," Bernadette said, staring at the door Cody held open.

This was turning out worse than she'd expected. How could she walk into Lakos Downtown with Cody by her side? Some of Grand Rapids' most influential businessmen ate lunch here. "Look, there's no need for you to spend a lot for lunch. I'm really not that hungry. Let's go back to that coffee shop near the store."

He continued holding the door open. "Eat as little or as much as you like. Don't worry about the cost."

Looking through the paned-glass window, she desperately groped for excuses. "You can see the bar's filled. There's probably a wait for tables."

"We won't know until we go in, will we?"

He didn't move, and his smile said he wasn't going to change his mind. Considering his earlier behavior, she didn't doubt he'd make a scene if she refused to go in, and with the patrons in the bar able to see them through the window, Bernadette decided to give up the battle.

"Oh, all right." She marched past him and into the wood-paneled hallway that led to the restaurant. All she could hope was that no one she knew was eating there today.

To her relief, Scott, the owner, wasn't there to greet them, and a waitress Bernadette had never seen before led them up the stairs to a booth. Every step of the way, Bern gritted her teeth, held her head high, and looked straight ahead. As soon as she was seated, she began reading her menu. Not once did she look around.

"It's okay," Cody said. "I'm sure no one will suspect we're having an affair."

The menu fell from her hands. "Affair?"

The word came out louder than she'd expected, and she quickly lowered her voice and picked up her menu again. "We are not having an affair, Mr. Taylor. We are not even having a—"

She stopped as a busboy approached to pour their water. All the while the young man was at the table, she smiled and pretended to study the menu. Internally her mind was racing, and the moment the busboy stepped away, she ground out her words. "I don't know what you're trying to prove, but I don't find this funny."

Calmly, Cody leaned back against the booth's dark green upholstered seat. "Have you ever heard the story 'The Golden Chain'?"

Destiny Unknown

"No." She glanced at the gold chain around his neck, and he touched it.

"My sister used to tell me the story when I was young. It's about three brothers. The two older brothers are smart and able. The younger is a dreamer and clumsy. They call him Dumb John and make fun of him all the time. But he has dreams that one day he will do something grand and noble."

"And of course he does," Bernadette said, trying to anticipate the point of his story.

"Of course." Cody grinned. "But not until he's a grown man. That's when he and his brothers go on a quest for a chain that will exactly fit their father's forge. The brother who comes back with the right size chain will inherit the father's blacksmith business. They have one month to succeed. One brother heads west, one east, and Dumb John heads north. Soon he comes across a green-skinned woman."

"Green skinned? Like little green men from Mars?"

"No, like an enchanted princess who's under a spell that can only be broken if someone sleeps in her cave three nights and doesn't speak a word between the hours of midnight and one."

"And naturally, our friend John volunteers." Bernadette could now see where the story was headed. She just didn't understand why Cody was telling it to her.

"John figures he's been called names all of his life and has had to keep quiet. Why not give it a try? So for three nights he sleeps in the cave, and between midnight and one, all manner of goblins and spirits come to the cave, some even impersonating him. And for three nights he resists saying anything, thus breaking the spell and turning the green-skinned woman back into a beautiful princess."

"And they live happily ever after."

"Not yet. There's still the matter of the golden chain."

"Ah yes, the golden chain." Again, her gaze went to the chain he wore. "One like that?"

"No, the one the princess gives Dumb John is big enough to go around a forge. You see, the princess marries Dumb John, making him a king, but when the end of the month comes, he remembers his original quest and knows his father and brothers will say he failed. Since the princess had promised to help him if he helped her, she gives him a special golden chain. He then puts on his torn and tattered clothing, takes the chain, and returns to his father's shop, where to his father's and brothers' surprise, the golden chain—and only the golden chain—fits the forge."

"Thus Dumb John takes over the business, dreams away the profits, and ends up going Chapter Eleven?"

Cody chuckled. "You're a cynic."

"So I've been told." It was safer than getting hurt. "Do you want to hear the end of this story or not?"

"I have a feeling I have no choice. So, how does the story end?"

"Well, Dumb John's brothers are jealous and throw him into a henhouse, where he stays until the princess shows up, looking for him."

"As usual, takes a woman to save the day."

Cody laughed. "I never thought of it that way."

"Being a man, you wouldn't. I can tell you, no woman would have gone back to work at a forge."

"Maybe not, but Dumb John had a point to prove. He needed to show his father and brothers that he wasn't dumb. And once the princess found him, he went back to their kingdom with her, but not before he again visited his father and brothers, this time dressed in his regal finery. It's said that after that, his brothers called themselves Dumb Will and Dumb Hans, and no one understood why."

"Cute." She pointed at his gold chain. "Does that mean you found your green princess?"

Cody grinned. "Well, I thought I had the other night."

Automatically she touched her forehead, remembering the green masque she'd started to put on Monday night. "I'm hardly a princess. Besides, you already have the golden chain."

"So I got ahead of myself."

His fairy tale was becoming more personal. "I don't need your help."

"Are you sure? You seemed very worried about some problems the other night."

"Minor disruptions at the store," she lied. "I simply want to make a good impression while the boss is away."

"You do seem very concerned about making a good impression."

"In my line of business, making a good impression is important."

"That's fine, as long as you don't lose sight of other things."

" 'Other things' such as the legality of the business?" They'd been over this before.

"Such as what's inside someone." Their waitress approached, and Cody nodded toward the woman. "Such as recognizing that everyone, no matter who she is or what she does, is important."

Quickly Bernadette retrieved her menu, made a choice, and gave her order. The moment the waitress left, Bernadette leaned toward Cody. "And what makes you think I don't feel she is important?"

"I think you rank people by their level of importance."

"I do not."

"Let's say you're walking along a street, and you see a car coming toward two men. One is clean shaven, dressed in a suit, and carrying a briefcase. The other one has long hair, is wearing baggy clothes, and looks like he hasn't washed for a month. You can only save one. Which one do you choose?"

"That's a ridiculous question."

"Is it?" He arched an eyebrow. "Or is it that you know the answer, and it makes you uncomfortable?"

"What makes me uncomfortable is a grown man trying to live out a fairy tale." There was the possibility he was crazy. Not that he acted like most of the flakes she'd met in her lifetime, but still . . . "Fairy tales are fantasies, Cody. Wishes. Your Dumb John was looking for respect. Is that what you want? A level of success and respectability?"

"No." He shook his head. "I'm perfectly satisfied with my level of success, and long ago I learned not to worry about how I look on the outside."

"Yet you judge others by how they look on the outside."

"What makes you say that?"

"Because the other day at the vet's office you looked at me and decided I was a snob."

"The way you were looking down your nose at me, that wasn't hard to do."

"Mine was a gut reaction to someone wearing very dirty clothes. Very dirty, I repeat."

Destiny Unknown
53

"In other words, the way I dress doesn't bother you?"

"Not at all," she lied.

"Good. Want to go out this weekend?"

She smiled. "No."

"Why not?"

She wasn't going to tell him her refusal had nothing to do with how he looked and everything to do with how he made her feel. A date with him would be dangerous. Volatile. Playing with fire. "I wouldn't want to waste your time. Unlike some, I don't believe opposites attract."

"And how do you know we're opposites?" The challenge was in his eyes, turning them a rich, alluring chocolate. "All you know about me is what you've judged from my appearance."

"And from what you've said. You like dogs; I don't. You don't care how you look; I do. You—"

Bernadette stopped. Walking toward their booth was none other than Frank Pierce, president of the True Fidelity Bank and Trust, one of the largest and most important banks in Grand Rapids. The man was on every influential committee in the city, and he and his wife had invited her to a select dinner party that weekend. If Cody had hoped to embarrass her, he was about to succeed. Having Frank see her in the company of a man who looked like the unemployment office was his second home was truly embarrassing.

She smiled as Frank neared, and tried to think of a way to explain her being with Cody. Frank returned her smile and gave a polite nod. Then he looked at Cody, and her stomach tightened into a knot. She could imagine what Frank was thinking.

"I thought that was you I saw going up the stairs," he said warmly.

To her surprise, he was speaking to Cody.

Cody looked up, grinned, and slid out of the booth. Instead of a handshake, the two men clasped each other's arms, and Bern watched, dumbfounded. Only after an exchange of pleasantries did Cody slip back into the booth, and Frank again acknowledged her presence.

"So, where did you meet this no-good roustabout?" he asked her.

Cody answered. "At the vet's office. Where else? Thor did it again. Cut his leg this time."

"That dog." Frank's laugh said he knew the problems Thor had encountered. "Of course," he added to Bernadette, "Cody's not much better. Watch out, Bern, that he doesn't fall down the stairs when you leave."

"Thanks, old buddy," Cody said, little sarcasm in his voice. "Build me up in the eyes of the lady."

"Trying to impress you, is he?" Frank said. "Talk to Marian. Cody drives her crazy. Yet she loves him. You should have heard them when he was working on our place. Bicker?" He shook his head. "It was comical."

"Cody worked on your house?" Bern asked. That explained their knowing each other.

"Basically did everything from designing it to pounding the final nail." Frank laughed. "He even helped us move in last month."

"Quite the man." She stared at Cody. He'd let her think he was an unemployed construction worker, had played to her expectations. Played her for a fool. "So, you're an architect?"

"No," he said. "My stepfather and stepbrothers are the architects. I never became one."

"Maybe not," Frank said, "but you're the one with

the ideas. Which reminds me. How's the new development coming along?"

"It's coming." Cody kept his gaze on her, not Frank. "I was checking out the property Monday."

"And will this new project be as successful as Devon Estates?" Frank asked.

"I hope so."

Once again Frank looked at Bernadette. "Hang on to your hat, gal. With Cody, you never know what to expect. The man's a genius. Totally unconventional, but a genius. You've got to see my new house."

"I will," Bernadette said to him. "I'll see it Friday night. Marian invited me to a dinner party you're having."

"Good." He nodded and stepped away. "Well, I guess I'd better get back to my table, let you two talk. Cody, why don't you stop by the bank sometime soon? I'd like to put a little money into this new development of yours."

Cody smiled up at him. "Always glad to take your money."

Bernadette waited until Frank had left before she faced Cody. His grin was as satisfied as the Cheshire cat's. She wanted to stuff a sock in his mouth. "You loved that, didn't you?"

Innocently he cocked his head. "Loved what?"

"Having Frank tell me you were rich and successful when you knew I thought you were some poor construction worker who couldn't afford a decent pair of jeans and needed a job."

"Frank never said I was rich and successful."

"Maybe not outright, but from what I've heard about Frank, he wouldn't be investing in your company if you weren't successful. You're the one who developed Devon

Estates?" She knew the area. Some of the store's wealthiest customers lived there.

"It's one of the projects I've worked on," he admitted.

"Worked on?" It seemed he was a man of understatement. "Like you 'worked' for Parker? 'I hammered a few nails.' That's what you said in the vet's office." She shook her head. "What did you really do for him?"

"Hammered a few nails. Cut a few boards." His eyes carried his grin. "I'm a developer. I take a project from start to finish, put together all the elements."

"In other words, you built his apartment building." A building she'd fallen in love with the moment she saw it. "But Parker said some company called DJ built his apartments."

Cody smiled. "That's the name of my company."

"DJ?"

"Dumb John."

"Of course." She got the message. Grabbing her purse, she slipped out of the booth and stood.

Cody frowned up at her. "Where are you going?"

"Back to the store. I seem to have lost my appetite."

"Don't be silly," he said, but slid out of the booth himself.

She was already headed for the stairs. Cody threw some money on the table and hurried after her. He caught up with her before she'd stepped outside. She glared at him when he held the door for her, and once on the sidewalk, she said nothing, just started for the store. He caught her arm. "We need to talk."

"About what?" The ice blue of her eyes would have frozen most men.

He wished it would cool his interest. "About us."

Destiny Unknown

"Us? There is no *us*. You like playing games, embarrassing people. I don't."

"I wasn't trying to embarrass you."

"Weren't you?" She looked down at his hand, gripping the sleeve of her coat. "Are you going to let me go?"

"If you insist."

He released his hold, expecting her to take off. She stayed where she was, glaring at him.

"Why?" she demanded. "Why dress like a bum? Pretend to be a common laborer?"

"I don't dress like a bum, I dress for comfort. And I am a common laborer." They were skirting the issue. "Look, I apologize. You made an assumption about me. I decided to let you think what you wanted."

She looked back toward the restaurant they'd just left. "You enjoyed every minute of that, didn't you?"

He wished he could deny it. He couldn't. "Frank's timing couldn't have been better."

"So, are you happy now? Now that you've humiliated me?"

The pain in her voice cut deep. He shook his head. "Humiliating you was never my purpose. All I wanted was for you to see that what's inside a person is more important than what's outside."

She let out her breath, the air turning to a misty cloud in the cold, and started toward the store. He fell into step beside her. "You're a beautiful woman. I can see where it would be difficult for you to understand how it feels to have people make fun of you because you're not pretty or smart or graceful."

Bernadette shot him a glance. "You have no idea what problems I've faced or how I feel."

"No, I guess I don't." He touched the gold chain

around his neck. Had he forgotten the reason he wore it, forgotten the lessons of his childhood? "So let's get to know each other better."

Stopping, she faced him. "Why? So you can humiliate me some more? You're right, you know. I do judge people on appearances. I would save the man in the suit. Are you going to start wearing a suit?"

"Suits don't last very long at construction sites."

"I don't imagine they do."

He lifted a hand, touching the side of her face with the backs of his fingers. Her skin was velvety soft. She shivered. "Cold?" he asked.

"A little."

"Come on, let's finish this conversation where it's warm." He slipped an arm around her shoulders, drawing her close, and walked with her toward the store.

Bernadette didn't want to finish the conversation. All she wanted was for Cody to go away. To disappear. He confused her. Disturbed her. He played games with her mind and with her emotions.

She walked by his side, praying he wouldn't guess the shaking was from nerves, not the cold, and her knees were threatening to buckle. This close to his body, his scent became a part of her, imprinting itself on her mind in a way she knew she would never forget. She wanted to hold on to her anger, to wipe him from her thoughts, but she knew neither was possible. How could she be angry with the truth? She'd judged him on first impressions, had snubbed him, and he'd played her for the fool she was.

She preferred walking away from a relationship; it gave her the control she'd never had as a child. She couldn't stop her father from going off and leaving her, not when she was growing up and not now, but she could protect herself against those feelings of desolation when it came to men. She had to protect herself now. In three brief encounters, Cody had affected her in ways she didn't like. Feelings she'd thought she could control had gotten out of control. Nothing was working out as it should.

He stayed close to her, warming her, confusing her, and exciting her, until they stepped through the doors to the store. Once inside, with warm air being blown down on them from the vents above, he stopped and turned her to face him. "So this is good-bye?"

It had to be, for her sake, though for some crazy reason she didn't want it to be. "Meeting you has been . . ." She groped for the right word. "Interesting."

He grinned. "Very interesting."

"I—" She licked her lips, her gaze locked on his eyes. Those tempting chocolate eyes.

She watched as his head came closer, and this time when his lips touched hers, she was prepared. This time his mouth lingered, playing over hers, tempting her and giving her a chance to feel the heat of his passion. This time she reached out, taking hold and capturing the heat. She gripped the leather of his jacket, her mouth moving against his. Control was forgotten. Good idea or not, she participated in the kiss. Wanted it. Needed it.

She was the one who resisted when he lifted his head. Only when a customer left the store, opening the outer door and letting in a blast of cold air, did Bernadette remember where she was. Quickly she released her hold on Cody's jacket.

"I've— We've—"

He touched a fingertip to her lips. "Good-bye, Princess."

FOUR

Bernadette figured it would be easy to forget Cody. He'd popped into her life. Now he could just pop out. Except it wasn't that easy. He kept popping up. In her thoughts, in her dreams, and in her daily conversations.

Over the next two days, three people mentioned Devon Estates and the man who'd developed that innovative community. He was called unusual, iconoclastic, and dogmatic. Those he'd butted heads with grumbled their comments, but all agreed, Cody Taylor built spectacular homes.

Knowing Cody had designed Marian and Frank Pierce's house, Bernadette was even more curious to see it. On Friday night she followed the directions Marian had given her, turned onto their paved drive, and gasped. Strategically situated on a knoll in Forest Hills, the house reigned over a frozen pond and snow-covered lawns, and reflected both the clean, orderly lines a banker would appreciate and a subtle elegance. The house also radiated a warmth that was repeated when Marian Pierce greeted Bernadette.

"I'm so glad you could come," she said, taking Bernadette's hands in hers. "I believe you already know some of our guests, but I'll introduce you around."

Marian was slightly shorter than Bernadette, but Bern had looked up to her from their first meeting. Here was the woman she wanted to be. Elegant, sophisticated, and wealthy. Marian's silk chemise, purchased at Morgan's, was a limited edition, stylish and subdued, its teal color a perfect complement for eyes as bright as sapphires and hair as rich as honey. Although it was common knowledge that the woman was pushing sixty, she didn't show the years. A personal trainer, good plastic surgeon, hair stylist, and expensive cosmetics—also purchased at Morgan's—saw to that.

She led Bernadette into a spacious living room where guests were standing and sitting in small groups. At a wet bar in the corner a bartender prepared drinks, while a woman in a white blouse and black skirt wandered through the room offering hors d'oeuvres. Bernadette recognized several of the people. It was a stuffy crowd, all of the guests influential in the local business community, and all reeking of money. Conversations were subdued, the atmosphere dignified.

Frank stood near a massive fireplace, talking to a middle-aged couple. He glanced her way, smiled and nodded, then went back to the discussion. Marian guided Bernadette toward the group.

Before they reached the fireplace, however, they were stopped by a man in his late thirties. He pushed himself up from a brocade chair, holding a drink in his right hand, his suit jacket unbuttoned. He positioned himself directly in front of them, blocking their progress. "Marian," he said, his gaze on Bernadette. "You certainly weren't going to parade this beautiful woman past me without an introduction, were you?"

Marian hesitated a moment, then smiled politely. "Of course not, Drew. Bernadette, I'd like you to meet Drew Bartlett. He's the market analyst for Dorff Finance. Drew, Bernadette Sanders. She's the—"

"General manager at Morgan's," Drew finished for her. He shifted his drink to his left hand and held out his right. "I've heard about you."

He wasn't a bad-looking man, perhaps a little overweight and probably not more than an inch or two taller than she was in heels. His fingers were limp and soft against hers, and cool from the drink he'd held. His gaze, however, was intense and slid down her body like heated oil. Immediately she didn't like him.

"You're here by yourself?" he asked.

Marian answered. "She's meeting someone."

It was news to Bernadette. "I am?"

"You are." Marian smiled. "And here he comes now." Her gaze moved to a point beyond Bernadette's left shoulder. "We were just talking about you, Cody."

"Were you?"

The sound of his voice switched every nerve cell in Bernadette's body onto alert. In a flash she recalled each of their meetings. The kisses they'd shared had been far too intimate, and an unbidden flush of color rushed to her cheeks. Keeping her expression neutral, she slowly turned to face him. "Imagine meeting you here."

He came up beside her. "Imagine."

On the surface she could control her emotions, but not inside. Cody's cocksure smile stirred butterflies in her stomach, and the look in his eyes provoked a tingling sensation even lower. Fighting the giddy feelings, she focused on his unconventional black suit. The cut was

Destiny Unknown

like nothing they carried at Morgan's. The jacket was slouchy yet trim, the lapels almost nonexistent, the double stitching so minute it barely showed. The pants softly hugged his hips, then tapered to break over black dress boots. Under the open jacket, he wore a brown striped vest and a natural-colored shirt with a banded collar. The fabrics were quality—the suit cashmere and the shirt linen—and she had to admit, the cut was perfect on him. In some circles his attire would be called fashionable, including the gold earrings, the gold chain, and the lack of a tie. In a room full of conservative business suits, he was a misfit.

"Ah, the Fitzpatricks have arrived," Marian said, and stepped away. "If you'll excuse me for just a minute. I have to relay a message from their babysitter."

Marian started toward the foyer, where a young couple had just been let in by the maid. Bernadette watched her leave, feeling abandoned.

"You're turning green on me again," Cody said.

If she'd known he was going to be there, she never would have worn the hunter green sheath. "What are you doing here?"

"I was invited."

"Or invited yourself." It made sense. He'd known from her conversation with Frank at the restaurant that she would be here tonight. Cody had undoubtedly called Marian after that. Which explained why Marian thought Bernadette was meeting him here.

He didn't deny her accusation, simply glanced Drew's way. "You'll have to excuse us," he said to the other man, "Bernadette and I are old friends."

"Old friends?" Bernadette heard her voice rise a notch. She could think of many words to describe their relationship. "Friends" was not one of them. "We've known each other a week. Less than a week."

"With some people there's an instant rapport."

"I'd hardly call what we have a rapport."

His smile widened. "Well, whatever."

"If you'll excuse me." Drew took a step back, his gaze darting between them.

Although Drew Bartlett was not a man who appealed to her, Bernadette wasn't about to let him leave her alone with Cody. "Actually, I'd like to talk to you, Mr. Bartlett . . . Drew." She stepped forward, smiling warmly as she slipped an arm through his. "What exactly does a market analyst do?"

"What do I do?" He glanced down at her arm, then back up at her face.

"How would you like to get me a drink?" She nodded toward the wet bar. "Then we can discuss the market here in Grand Rapids."

"Sounds good to me."

Cody watched them walk away, Drew tossing back a triumphant smile. He knew what Bernadette was doing, but if she thought he cared who she went off with, she was wrong. Ever since leaving her at the entrance to Morgan's two days ago, he'd been lecturing himself on the stupidity of being interested in her. It was great that she was going off with another man. Eliminated temptation.

So what if she looked absolutely drop-dead gorgeous or that she was dressed in green. She wasn't an enchanted princess from a fairy tale. She wasn't a princess at all, unless it was an ice princess.

He had to remember that.

"You let her get away?"

Cody turned at the sound of Marian's voice. She'd

returned to his side and was watching Drew Bartlett get Bernadette a drink.

"What are you up to, Marian?"

She smiled. "Nothing, my dear. Absolutely nothing at all."

"You want to explain why you invited me?"

Her expression turned innocent. "So my guests could meet the man who designed my house. What other reason would I have?"

"As I recall, when you phoned, you said you wanted me to meet someone."

"You know me, always trying to introduce you to the right people." She continued smiling, her gaze switching back to Drew and Bernadette. "At the time, I didn't know you already knew her."

"At the time, I didn't."

"She'll find him obnoxious," Marian said. "I didn't even want Frank to invite him, but Frank said he owed him."

"Got to keep the sheet balanced." Cody had heard that often enough from his stepfather.

"You're such a cynic." Marian glanced his way, then looked back at Drew. "It's bad enough that he ogles every woman around. Tonight he arrived half-stewed. Seems his date backed out at the last minute." She laughed softly, her words too low for others to hear. "The woman must have been smarter than Drew realized. Anyway, Frank told the bartender to water down his drinks, but every time I look, Drew's back at the bar."

"Think he'll become a problem?" One thing Cody had learned from being married to an alcoholic, drinking eroded good judgment.

"I believe he already is. He's stealing your woman."

Cody shook his head. "She's not my woman."

"And those sparks I saw the moment she looked at you? I suppose you're going to deny them."

"You have a good imagination."

Marian smiled. "You'd make an interesting couple."

"We're total opposites."

"Opposites attract."

"Or repel." A fact Bernadette had made clear. "How long have you known her?"

"Five months. We met at a party Parker put on to introduce her around. Bern and I clicked immediately, not that we see each other that often. Up until a month ago, simply keeping an eye on you so you didn't do anything too radical with this house kept me busy." Her smile was in her eyes.

"If the two of you clicked, that should tell you she's not a good match for me."

"She's a perfect match. Someone to keep you in line." She poked a long, painted nail against the front of his shirt. "Frank said she walked out on you the other day."

Cody smiled. "Seems I said something she didn't like."

"Well, see if you can say things she'll like during dinner. She'll be seated next to you."

"Marian?"

Smiling, Marian walked away.

Bernadette tried to stay focused on what Drew Bartlett was saying, but her gaze continually drifted to Cody, in part because he'd positioned himself so that he was always in her view, and in part because what Drew was saying was so boring. Even her economics instructors at

Destiny Unknown

Western had been more interesting. And how a man could talk and down so many drinks was beyond her. Within an hour Drew had managed three Scotch and sodas to her one glass of wine.

She was relieved when the maid stepped into the living room and announced that dinner was served. Her relief, however, was short-lived when the seating arrangement was announced. Cody's smug smile said he'd known they'd be next to each other. Drew complained about being seated at the end of the table, away from Bernadette, reminding her of a spoiled brat. She hoped he was pleased when Marian accommodated his wishes. Bernadette wasn't. Now she had Cody on her left and Drew on her right. It was bound to be a delightful dinner.

Seated across from her were the Fitzpatricks. Marian had introduced them earlier. Rick Fitzpatrick was a vice president at Frank's bank. The youngest. His wife, Patti, hadn't gone back to work after the birth of their first child, and she was now five months pregnant with their second. Bernadette guessed both husband and wife to be in their late twenties. Ignoring the two men seated beside her, she spoke to Patti. "We're thinking of making some changes at Morgan's. What's your impression of the maternity wear selection?"

Rick answered for his wife. "Must be good. I swear Patti would spend all of our money at Morgan's if I'd let her."

Patti pointed at the dress she had on. "I bought this there. What I like is the variety you offer."

Bernadette tried to concentrate on Patti's comments, not on the fingers snaking down the side of her left leg. She'd had men grope her before, but this was ridiculous.

Feather light, the touch of Cody's hand triggered unbidden responses. She moved her leg.

"What *is* he doing?" Patti asked, trying to peer over the table without getting up.

Bernadette glared at Cody, but all she could see was the back of his jacket and the top of his head near her thigh. Then he straightened, smiling as he sat back in his chair.

"Dropped it." He held up his napkin for all to see, his smile innocent.

Bernadette didn't believe for a moment that the napkin had been dropped accidentally or that Cody's hand had just happened to brush against her leg.

"Problem?" Drew asked, leaning forward to look at Cody.

"No problem," Cody assured him. "Just retrieving something I'd lost. Right, Princess?"

"I'm not your princess."

"Of course not."

Cody straightened his chair, shook out his napkin, and flamboyantly placed it across the front of his trousers. Bernadette tried not to pay any attention. Smiling politely, she prayed no one thought she was with him.

Once he was settled, she thought she could relax, but soon realized she was wrong. Somehow he'd managed to position his chair closer to hers. His sleeve now touched her bare arm, and though she was sure others couldn't see it, she could feel him move his arm ever so slightly, the soft cashmere of his jacket sleeve tickling and caressing her skin and sending shivers down her spine. Needing an escape, she inched closer to Drew.

Once more, Cody reached down between them, his hand touching her leg. "Napkin slipped again," he said. Once again he pulled it back onto his lap.

"Perhaps you should tie it around your neck," she said, keeping her voice low.

"Perhaps." His grin was pure mischief.

"He could loop it through that necklace he wears," Drew said loudly.

Cody didn't respond, just kept smiling.

"You like dressing like a girl?" Drew goaded.

Cody leaned forward, and Bernadette tensed. Reaching under the table, she touched his knee. Cody looked at her, winked, and said nothing.

"Pretty dumb to come to a formal dinner party without a tie, if you ask me," Drew continued. "And what is it with that jacket? Your tailor run out of material when he got to the lapels?"

Through her fingers Bernadette could feel the tensing of Cody's muscles. Drew was looking for a fight. There was no question about it.

It was Frank Pierce who put an end to the confrontation. Pushing back his chair, he stood and raised his glass. "I'd like to propose a toast." He nodded at Cody. "To the man who created this house."

Throughout the meal Bernadette maintained a smile and a straight back and wondered how she swallowed a bite. When Drew wasn't throwing barbs at Cody, he was making suggestive remarks to her. With Cody, it was his silence that unnerved her. Oh, he answered questions the other guests asked about the house and his various projects, but he said nothing to Drew and little to her.

Which should have been fine. They'd said all that needed to be said. They were opposites, two ships passing in the night. Why pretend otherwise?

She was sure it was the awkward situation that had

her stomach tied in knots. Tension was the reason for her rapid pulse, not Cody's occasional smiles. And so what if her skin tingled every time his sleeve brushed her arm. She was simply sensitive.

After dinner, when Frank suggested the women take a tour of the house while he showed the men his game room, Bernadette sighed with relief. She'd had her fill of men for one evening. Once she'd seen the house, she was going to make her excuses and leave. After that, she hoped she never ran into Cody Taylor or Drew Bartlett again.

Before she had a chance to move, however, Drew had his hand on her arm. "What do you say we split now?"

"Split?" She pretended ignorance. "I don't understand."

"Go to my place . . . or yours." He grinned. "Get to know each other better."

She felt Cody touch her leg. Quickly she glanced his way. She knew by the look in his eyes that he was offering his assistance. She didn't want his help, and shook her head before looking back at Drew. As coolly as she could, she gave him her answer. "Not interested."

"Right." Drew continued grinning.

Pushing back her chair, she stood. "If you'll excuse me, I'm going to use the powder room, then I'm going on a tour of the house. And then I'm going home. Alone."

She emphasized the last word before walking over to Marian. Marian directed her to the bathroom off the master bedroom, and Bernadette headed up the stairs. More than physical relief, she needed emotional relief. A few minutes to herself. Time to settle the rapid beat of her heart and compose her thoughts.

Destiny Unknown

71

Monday night she'd been thinking she needed to get out more. Well, tonight was enough to remind her of the pitfalls of dating. There were always the Drew Bartletts of the world. They drank too much, got obnoxious, and caused more trouble than they were worth.

There were also plenty of Cody Taylors in the world, the rebels who liked to stir things up. She'd managed to avoid them in the past. And with good reason, she realized. Being around them was just too dangerous.

Cody was proof of that. He'd said little and yet had kept her emotions in a turmoil all evening. He was driving her crazy.

In the bathroom she looked around and knew one thing for certain. Much as she might want to avoid Cody, she did like the homes he designed. Standing in front of the vanity, she could feel as well as see the warmth and elegance of the room. "Taylor made," she said aloud, and smiled at the words. Next thing she knew, she'd be advertising for him.

She still hadn't put Cody out of her thoughts when she stepped back into Frank and Marian's bedroom. To her surprise, Drew was standing in the middle of the room. "Next?" she asked, waving a hand toward the bathroom door.

Drew stepped toward her. "I hope I'm first. At least, tonight."

She didn't understand, not until his hands were on her shoulders and he was pulling her to him. "What the—?"

"I'm tired of being stood up, of women thinking they can jerk me around. First Sue, now you."

"Sue?" He was pushing her back, and Bernadette resisted. "I don't—" Her heel caught on the thick pile of the carpeting, and she struggled to keep her balance.

Drew's weight was to his advantage, and he half lifted, half dragged her backward until she felt her legs hit something soft and knew they'd reached the edge of Marian and Frank's king-sized bed.

She started to scream, but Drew shoved a hand over her mouth, his pudgy fingers blocking her nose. She twisted her head, struggling for breath. "Stop fighting me," he ordered, scowling down at her. "You know you want this. You've been after me all night."

She tried to deny it, to push him off. His weight held her against the mattress, her struggles only twisting her dress higher on her thighs. She felt Drew's hand sweeping up her leg and strained to clamp her thighs together, fear grabbing her mind.

And then suddenly he was off her.

"Get out."

It was all Cody said, but Drew didn't hesitate. With barely a glance toward her, he headed for the door. Only when he was in the hallway did he let loose with a string of swear words. Cody took a step toward him, and Drew scurried out of sight.

She watched Cody, saw the tension slowly leave his body and his fists relax. She couldn't explain the emotions coursing through her. Relief. Adoration.

Embarrassment.

Before he turned toward her, she pushed herself off the bed, straightening her dress and pulling it back down to her knees. Over and over, she rubbed her hands across her front, remembering the feel of Drew's hands on her and the weight of his body. He'd smelled of Scotch and lust, and she tried to wipe the memory away.

"You okay?" Cody asked, his voice soft.

"Fine." The word came out tight. She couldn't seem to breathe, couldn't get the feel of those hands off her.

Destiny Unknown

"Bern?"

She looked at him, but his face blurred as tears filled her eyes. She bit down on her lower lip, needing to hold on to some control. She wouldn't cry.

"It's all right." Cody held out his arms, and without a word she stepped into his embrace, pressing her face against his shirt. "It's all right," he repeated, and she gave in and let the tears come.

Crying wasn't her style. She wasn't the weepy type. So she'd been attacked. Nothing had happened. She was acting like a fool, and she was getting Cody's shirt wet.

One minute. That's all she would take. Just a minute to let her heartbeat slow and the fear wash away. One minute to enjoy the security of Cody's arms and the strength of his presence.

Except she didn't have a minute. She heard Marian's voice in the distance, explaining the features of her new house. Getting louder. Closer.

In a moment Marian would be coming through the doorway and into the bedroom.

Bernadette didn't wait. She pulled Cody toward the bathroom. "Quick. In here."

Cody watched Bernadette lock the bathroom door. Her eyes were still glistening with tears, her cheeks still flushed when she placed a finger against her lips, asking for silence. He heard the women enter the bedroom, Marian describing the decisions that had gone into the design of that room. All he could think was, thank goodness they hadn't designed a lock on the bedroom door. He hated to imagine what might have happened if Drew had locked that door. Hated to think what might have happened if he'd gone with Frank instead of deciding to talk to Bernadette.

The doorknob to the bathroom turned, and Bernadette sucked in a breath. "Is someone in there?" Marian called from the other side.

"Me," Bernadette said, her voice shaky.

"I wondered where you were. I thought maybe you'd decided to take off." Marian's tone became concerned. "Are you all right?"

"Fine . . . I'm fine," Bernadette said, though her voice cracked. "I—I just need a few more minutes."

"You're sure you're all right? We saw Drew coming down the stairs. He seemed upset."

"Probably . . . probably because I was in here. I told him to try the one downstairs."

Cody admired Bernadette's quick thinking. The question was, did Marian buy the excuse? For a moment she said nothing, then asked, "Do you want us to wait?"

"No." The word sounded too desperate, but Bernadette quickly continued. "I mean, there's no need. I'll—I'll catch up with you."

"You're sure?" There was another hesitation before Marian went on. "You haven't seen Cody, have you?"

"Cody?" Bernadette looked his way. "No. Why?"

"Frank was looking for him."

"I'm sure he's around somewhere." Her gaze never left his face, her eyes saying more than her words. "He has a way of showing up when you least expect it."

"Well, if you need anything," Marian went on, "let me know. We'll be in the next room."

Bye-bye, Cody mouthed, and waved at the closed door. Then he looked back at Bernadette. It was going to take more than a minute before she could face others.

From the built-in storage shelf he'd designed, he

Destiny Unknown

grabbed one of Marian's wash cloths. He dampened it with cool water and handed it to Bernadette. "For your eyes."

She stared into the mirror. "I look a sight."

"You look beautiful."

The sidelong glance she gave him said she didn't believe him. "How can I thank you?"

"You don't have to. Always got to rescue the princess. It's a given."

"Back to that fairy tale?" She managed a smile. "Was this Dumb John to the rescue?"

He grinned and tweaked her nose. "You got it, gal. And now I think Dumb John better get out of here before he's discovered *in* the john."

He was gone as quickly as he'd appeared, and Bernadette stared into the vanity mirror, wondering what had happened to her staid, controlled life. Her hair was a mess, her cheeks flushed, and her lipstick smeared. Quickly she pinned her hair back into place and applied a fresh coat of lipstick.

Just as she stepped out of the bathroom she heard men yelling and the squeal of tires. By the time she reached the bedroom door, Marian and the other women were coming out of the next room. They all headed down the stairs and to the front door.

Bernadette stepped outside with the others, shivering in the cold night air. The men were already gathered around a red truck. As she neared, she saw the lettering on the side. *DJ Development*. She also saw that its windshield was shattered, and Cody was kneeling by the front fender, running a fingertip through a stream of green liquid. "He punctured the radiator," he said, and slowly rose to his feet.

"I saw him do it," Rick Fitzpatrick said. "I couldn't

believe it. He parked his car next to your truck, got something out of his trunk, and started pounding away at your radiator and windshield."

"Looked like a sledgehammer to me," one of the other men said.

"I didn't know where you were," Rick went on. "But the moment I opened the door, he jumped back into his car and took off. The guy's gotta be crazy."

Frank shook his head. "I knew he'd had too much to drink, and that there was no love lost between you two, but I never thought he'd do anything like this. What could have set him off?"

Bernadette felt Cody's gaze burn through her, and she held her breath. He shook his head. "Who knows."

"I'll call 911," Marian said, and started back into the house.

"And we'll make sure you get a ride home," Frank assured Cody. "And your truck fixed."

"I'll drive him home," Bernadette said firmly.

FIVE

One hour later Bernadette drove her car away from Frank and Marian's house, Cody seated next to her. The police had been called, the incident rehashed, and goodbyes said. All she wanted to do was drop Cody off at his house, go home, and forget the night had ever happened.

As if she ever could.

She turned off the driveway and onto the street before she said anything. Although she'd been mentally practicing for over an hour, her apology came out shaky, and she didn't look his way. "I'm sorry about your truck."

"No need to be sorry. It wasn't your fault." He touched her arm, the mellow tone of his voice like a balm.

She glanced down at the hand resting on her sleeve, then at him. In the darkness she could barely make out his silhouette. Her heart racing, she returned her gaze to the road. "We both know it was my fault. If you hadn't come into the bedroom when you did, hadn't stopped him, he wouldn't have bashed in your windshield and radiator."

"Bern, you are not responsible for him acting like an animal."

Again she glanced his way. "I led him on."

"You talked to him. You didn't lead him on."

"Before dinner I was flirting with him." To upset Cody. It seemed so childish now. "I obviously took it too far. I'll pay for the repairs to your truck."

"If Barlett doesn't pay for the damages, my insurance company will."

"I owe you something for what you did."

"You're giving me a ride home."

"As if—" She slowed at a stop sign. Perhaps it was better to leave things as they were. "Which way?"

"Turn left."

She followed his directions to a part of Forest Hills she hadn't driven through before, her thoughts in a jumble. All evening she'd tried to avoid Cody, and here she was taking him home. Every time she thought she understood him, she discovered a new side. He wasn't her type, but she had to admit, he had some very good qualities. Prince Charming had come to her rescue.

It was crazy.

He pointed toward a mailbox by the side of the road. "Turn there."

She turned onto a paved drive that led into a grove of pines. The enchanted forest? she wondered. How far had he taken his fairy tale? Would his house be a castle?

Once through the trees, she laughed. Straight ahead was his house, and it was anything but a castle.

"You laugh?" He chuckled himself. "My stepfather always said I'd end up living in a shack, so I decided to prove him right."

Destiny Unknown

"A shack," she repeated. The structure in front of her did look like a shack, as if a bunch of boards had been randomly nailed together to form an oversized, not quite plumb clubhouse.

The longer she looked, though, the more she saw. Although the boards of mixed widths and wood grains appeared to be put together haphazardly, they actually created a subtle design of texture and shape, color and tone. And though the windows were set at varying angles, defying common tradition, and the outside edges of the house were not even, the house wasn't about to fall over. It simply did not fit architectural terms such as colonial, Cape Cod, or Queen Anne.

"Would you like to see the inside?" Cody asked.

Bernadette didn't hesitate. "Yes."

Even the stone steps leading up to the front door were different, no two alike. "They come from all over Michigan," he explained. "Farmers are always glad to let you clean out their fields."

"I imagine. And the door?" She pulled off a glove and touched the bas-relief carvings in smooth dark wood. Flora, fauna, and figures filled six squares. The panels told a story, one she now knew, of a man, a princess, and a gold chain.

"A friend created this door," he said. "If you'll note . . ." He touched a central figure, the wood stained green.

"Your green princess." Bernadette eyed him curiously. "And once I step through this door, will your shack be transformed into a castle?"

"I suppose that depends on your definition of castle." He opened the door.

Cody's house wasn't a castle, not by her definition, but it certainly wasn't a shack. Two stories high, open and airy, it had modern recessed lighting, an intercom system, and a computer that welcomed him home in a sexy female voice. It was the traditional that was missing, and she could just imagine the decorating department at Morgan's trying to figure out how to handle windows and walls set at non-right angles.

In many cases, Cody had solved the problem by doing nothing. His windows were not covered, and natural woods were allowed to express their own beauty. Floors were wood or slate or carpeted, sometimes all three in the same room. An uneven clicking sound caught her attention, and she looked to her right. Cody's German shepherd came limping out of the kitchen.

The mud was gone, the dog's coat a healthy combination of tans and charcoal grays, and the underwear that had been wrapped around his leg had been replaced by a neat bandage. She tried to remember the dog's name.

"How you doing, Thor?" Cody knelt and rubbed his dog's head. "Do you remember Bernadette?"

As if recognizing her, Thor wagged his tail and started toward her. His size alone was frightening, but she resisted an impulse to step back, and tentatively held out her hand to let the dog sniff it. When Thor began sniffing at the hem of her coat as well, she did step back.

Cody noticed her reaction. "He won't hurt you. I swear, if a robber came in, Thor would show him around."

"So why do you keep him?"

Cody wondered if a woman who didn't like dogs would understand. "He's my buddy." Looking over at the computer monitor mounted on the wall, Cody called out a command. "All lights on."

Bernadette's surprised "Oh" when the lights

Destiny Unknown

throughout the house came on was one of pleasure. He took off his overcoat and hooked it on a peg by the door. "This is it, my vision of home sweet home. My castle, I suppose you could say."

As far as rooms went, there weren't many. He hadn't seen a need for a formal dining room, separate laundry room, or lots of bedrooms. On the main floor was an entryway with a staircase going up to the second floor, a kitchen, a small bathroom, and a huge expanse that served as his living room, office, and gym. He watched as Bernadette walked over to the kitchen. Without going in, she looked through the doorway, then turned to look across the entryway.

To Cody's left was a massive fireplace made of the same stones as the steps outside. Facing the fireplace was a mixture of furniture and floor pillows. Beyond them was an assortment of plants, a fifty-gallon aquarium, and his desk. It was the far section of the room that he enjoyed the most. The basketball hoop hanging on the wall was used for games of one-on-one, and a net could be strung across the middle of the area for volleyball or badminton. On the wooden floor he sometimes drew squares for hopscotch and circles for marbles. Physical exercise, he'd learned, kept the body fit and the ideas flowing. His best designs had come when he was having fun, and in the winter it was nice to have space to play inside.

Bernadette studied the area in silence, then turned and looked at his staircase. "And up there?"

"My bedroom, a bathroom, and a spare bedroom. My room is a mess."

She grinned. "Why doesn't that surprise me?"

He watched her start up the stairs. Thor went, too, bumping his way past Bernadette to be first at the land-ing. With the two of them going, Cody saw no alternative but to follow.

Thor went straight to his favorite place by the bed and plopped down with a sigh, laying his head on the suit jacket Cody had tried on earlier that evening, then had dropped on the floor. Looking at his unmade bed, covered with an assortment of jackets, shirts, and ties, Cody knew Bernadette was seeing more than he'd wanted her to know. He tried to make light of it. "I can never decide what to wear to one of Frank and Marian's dinner parties."

Bernadette looked at him, her gaze drifting down over the suit he'd finally chosen. "It's different, but on you it looks good."

Stepping into the room, she went over to his bed, lifted one of the discarded jackets, studied it, then let it fall back onto the bed. "Marian said she invited you two weeks ago."

She didn't look at him, and he supposed that was as much of an apology as he would get in regard to her earlier snide comments. It was more than he'd expected. "Marian thinks I need to be more sociable. She's always trying to connect me with the right people."

Bernadette wandered over to the triangular window facing the field behind his house. "She says you can really be irritating."

He smiled, remembering some of the arguments he'd had with Marian. "Our opinions sometimes differ."

Facing him again, Bernadette walked toward him. "What she said was, 'He's a pain in the butt, but nice.' She also said you were raised in California and had a rough childhood."

He shrugged and stepped back into the hallway, giving her room to exit his bedroom. He didn't want to talk about his childhood.

She stopped in front of him. "So rough you left California for Michigan?"

"I was the brother who headed north, remember?"

"And your brothers headed east and west?"

"Stepbrothers," he corrected her. "And yes. One lives about five miles west of my stepfather's house, and the other lives twenty miles east."

"And your sister?"

Cody was surprised she had remembered Karen. He especially didn't want to talk about his sister, though. "She died."

"I'm sorry."

It was an automatic response, one he was used to hearing. Turning away, he walked over to a closed door and opened it. "This is the spare bedroom, but as you'll note, it's not used as that."

The room was filled with boxes that contained drafting supplies and files, books, and building equipment. Anything and everything that needed to be kept safe and dry was stored in the room. He planned on building a storage area outside for some of the equipment. He just hadn't gotten to it yet.

"Next is the bathroom."

He led her to the last room on the second level and stepped inside. Bernadette followed, Thor by her side, his toenails clicking over the slate floor. The bathroom was enormous, as big as an average living room. There was the usual tub, shower, and sink. What was different was the sunken whirlpool that took up a third of the space. The dog went over and sniffed the water.

"Thor," Cody warned, and the dog looked back at him, his tail wagging.

"He thinks it's his private drinking bowl," Cody explained. "Problem is, he sometimes falls in, and the dumb dog can't swim. Plus I then have to filter out the dog hair."

She laughed, the sound warm and relaxed. "I told you dogs were messy."

"But lovable." Thor had come back to her side, and Cody watched Bernadette rub the dog's head. He had a feeling she wasn't even aware of the gesture.

"It's nice." She glanced around the room. "All in all, a very interesting shack, Mr. Taylor."

"Keeps the rain off my head."

She walked back out into the hallway, and he followed. "So, tell me," he said as she headed for the stairs. "What would your dream house look like?"

She walked beside him down the stairs, taking each step slowly. "To tell you the truth, I don't know. I've never really thought about owning a house. A condominium, yes. In fact, just last month I talked to a realtor about what's available."

"We're going to design some condos into this new development I'm working on. Maybe you could give me some ideas what a woman of your income and education is looking for."

He stopped halfway to his front door and glanced toward the kitchen. Bernadette had been giving him lots of ideas all evening, none good for his sanity. The one that had just popped into his head was crazy. Insane. But . . .

"Would you like something to drink?" he asked. "Coffee, tea or . . ." He grinned. "Hot chocolate?"

Bernadette knew she should leave. She'd brought him home, had seen his house, and had thanked him for saving her from possibly being raped. Now was the time

Destiny Unknown

to say "Good-bye, it was nice meeting you but we have nothing in common, it wouldn't go anywhere, and why waste our time."

Except she didn't want to say good-bye. Maybe it was the house she didn't want to leave. So totally unlike anything she'd ever seen before, it fascinated her. Or maybe it was the man who fascinated her. "Hot chocolate sounds good."

"Two hot chocolates coming up." He helped her out of her coat, hanging it next to his.

"You picked a drink I couldn't resist," she said, rubbing her hands together and feeling uncommonly nervous. "I think I'm addicted to chocolate."

Cody faced her, and she looked into eyes the color of milk chocolate. Her insides turned queasy, and she knew she'd made a mistake in saying she would stay. Chocolate wasn't good for her, and neither was Cody Taylor.

"My ex loved Godiva chocolates," he said, and led the way into his kitchen. "Godiva chocolates and bourbon."

"Well, I like the Godiva chocolates, but not with bourbon."

"I'll have to remember that."

She didn't want him remembering her likes and dislikes. She didn't want him thinking about her . . . or herself thinking about him. She especially didn't want her pulse racing, but that was exactly what it was doing. All because he'd stopped by a chair and had slipped off his jacket . . . then his vest. He was rolling up the sleeves of his shirt, exposing the muscles of his forearms and the dark hairs that covered them, and she was trying to look blasé about the whole thing while butterflies were doing somersaults in her stomach.

"So what does a single woman with a good job and a

concern with outward appearances want"—he looked her way—"in a condominium?"

"Want?" She smiled, the answer forming in her head. *You.*

By the time Cody carried their mugs of cocoa out of the kitchen and over to the fireplace, Bernadette had given him some ideas about what she liked in living space and had learned quite a bit about him. She knew he'd built his "shack" ten years earlier, that his ex-wife had almost gotten it in their divorce settlement, and then, at the last minute, had agreed to a large cash settlement. In addition to being able to control the lights with voice commands, he could request music, raise or lower the heat, and turn on the television. She was surprised when he said no one in his family had ever stepped foot in the place. "As far as my stepfather and brothers are concerned, I'm an incompetent klutz who shouldn't have succeeded as a developer. They are so stuck in the traditional, that even if they did come here, they wouldn't have a good word to say about anything I've done. Not that it matters what they think. As for my mother—" He shrugged. "She chose sides a long time ago."

Bernadette heard the regret in his voice. "How old were you when your father died? Your real father."

Cody began stacking kindling in the fireplace. "I was two."

"And when your mother married your stepfather?"

"Seven." He shook his head. "She finally had her dream man. Never mind that she thrust her children into a living nightmare."

"You make it sound terrible."

"For Karen and me, it was. You see, we were Char-

Destiny Unknown

lie's kids, and Charlie Taylor had stolen our mother's heart when she was in college. Stole her right out from under Bill Pardue's nose.

"Bill didn't waste any time before he got married himself and had two sons, Keith and Kevin, but I guess he never got over Mom. By the time I came along, Mom had realized she'd married the wrong man, that Charlie Taylor was a good-looking dreamer who would never give her the money or prestige she wanted. When my father died in a factory accident, Bill was working in Europe. I'll admit, life wasn't easy for Mom. Money was tight and we had to move in with Grandma Cody. We lived with her for four years, then Bill Pardue moved back to town. Within a year he'd divorced his wife, gotten custody of his boys, and married my mother. At last they were together."

"And you and your sister were the outcasts," she said, understanding.

"You got it. Keith and Kevin picked on us from day one. It was as if their father's hatred of our father and us had been transferred genetically to them. We couldn't do anything right."

"And your mother?"

"Had the life she'd always wanted, so she pretended it wasn't happening, that everything was fine. She's still pretending."

"When was the last time you saw her?"

"Not that long ago, actually. Twelve months next week." He built a nest of the kindling. "I go back once a year to visit my sister's grave. Because I'm dumb, I stop in and see my mother."

"Was your sister older or younger?"

"Older. Karen was six when I was born. She was my little mommy. My protector. She'd tell me not to listen to my stepbrothers, tell me it didn't matter if they called us dumb, that one day we would show them."

"Just like Dumb John in the story."

"Exactly. She even gave me this gold chain for my high school graduation"—he touched the chain around his neck—"as a reminder. Problem was, she didn't listen to her own advice. Like you, she cared what others thought and said about her, and that made her vulnerable to them."

Cody lit a match, and a wad of crumpled paper ignited the kindling. In silence he stared at the flames.

Bernadette also watched the fire. There was a question she had to ask. "How did she die?"

He sighed. "She stopped trying to please them."

"She took her own life?"

"Took it. Gave it away." Cody shrugged, his gaze locked on the fire. "I didn't like being called dumb and having them laugh at me, but it just made me stronger. With Karen, the need to please ate away at her self-confidence. The irony was, she reached the end of her endurance the night she should have been celebrating. She got a promotion. An office of her own. A big raise and stock options. Instead of opening a bottle of champagne, she opened a bottle of pills. One of her friends found her the next day."

Bernadette closed her eyes. The pain and anguish in his voice cut through her too. "How old were you at the time."

"Nineteen."

In college. She understood him better now. He wasn't a rebel without a cause. Every stand he made was for his sister.

She felt his hand on her arm. "Enough about me.

What about you, Bern? I don't want you feeling guilty about what happened at Frank and Marian's."

She opened her eyes. He'd moved next to her and was studying her face. She had a feeling he wanted to change the subject . . . needed to change it. And she needed to thank him. "It's difficult not to feel guilty, but I also feel very lucky. I don't know why you came to my rescue after the way I'd been treating you all night, but I'm glad you did."

"Strange how things happen." He shifted his body down onto the thick wool throw rug in front of the hearth, his head suddenly lower than hers. Reaching back, he grabbed his mug of cocoa. "I kept telling myself to leave you alone, stop pestering you."

Staring into his mug, he laughed. "Thing is, I couldn't stop. Pestering you was too much fun."

"Glad I gave you some amusement."

She didn't sound glad, Cody thought, and the sight he'd encountered when he'd stepped into that bedroom hadn't been fun or amusing. Seeing Bernadette on the bed and Drew Bartlett over her had raised his protective instincts and more. Maybe nothing could come of a relationship between them, but that didn't stop him from wanting her or from thinking of her as his.

Thor came in from the kitchen and curled up beside him, laying his head on his lap. Absently, Cody scratched between the dog's ears, hoping Thor didn't grace them with one of his late night gifts. "Lights low," he commanded, and the lights dimmed, the room taking on a dusky glow. "Okay, I've told you about my family. Now it's your turn to tell me about yours."

"There's not a lot to tell." She moved to sit beside him on the rug. "I have one sister, Effie, who's two years my junior and is a clown—literally. She's now married to

Parker Morgan, whom she's loved since she was in her teens. You lost your father. We lost our mother. She died when I was seven and Effie was five. From that time on, we were raised by our grandparents. We see our father usually two or three times a year. Otherwise he's over in Egypt digging up old bones and broken pieces of pottery or traveling around the world, giving lectures."

"He's an archeologist?"

"Uh-huh." She reached over to where she'd set her purse. "I have a recent picture of him at one of the digs. He gave it to me when he was here for Effie's wedding."

Cody looked at the snapshot. It showed a man kneeling in front of an assortment of pottery fragments. He was lean and tanned from the sun, his face was wrinkled, and his hair was mostly gray, with just a tinge of red. Cody glanced up at Bernadette. "I see a little resemblance, but not much."

"My sister takes after his side of the family. Everyone says I look like my mother."

"Are you close to him?"

"How close can you get to a man you rarely see, who drops in and out of your life?"

Her wistful expression touched Cody, and he found it ironic. "You'd like to be closer to your father; I'm glad to be far away from my stepfather." He handed back the picture. "Actually, we have a lot in common. We both lost a parent, grandparents played a part in our childhood, and the one remaining parent has more or less deserted us, yours for artifacts and mine for a man who will give her the lifestyle she most desires."

Bernadette stared at the picture of her father. "So why do we care?"

"Good question." And one he didn't have an answer

for, so he changed the subject. "What were your grandparents like?"

She looked at him, a smile replacing her melancholy. "Nice. Loving. Kind of old-fashioned and not very cultured. That I've had to teach myself."

"And how do you teach yourself culture?"

"By going to concerts and plays, the ballet. When I was in college, I attended anything and everything I could afford to buy a ticket for or could talk someone into taking me to."

He wasn't sure if she realized what she was doing, but she'd reached over and was running a fingertip across the top of Thor's head, which was still resting in Cody's lap. When she slid her fingers down the side of the dog's head and into the ruff around his neck, it wasn't just the dog she was stroking. Immediately, Cody felt a tightening in his crotch, a jolt of desire shooting through his loins. He held his breath, afraid to move. Saying nothing, he swallowed hard.

Bernadette went on talking, either not realizing what she was doing or more audacious than he'd suspected. "I remember trying to get Parker to like opera," she said, and laughed softly. "That was a losing proposition. And he absolutely refused to go to the ballet with me. Did you know I went with Parker when I was a teenager?"

Cody shook his head, afraid to talk.

She nodded and went back to stroking Thor's head and neck. "Parker and I dated for three years. Broke up the year I graduated from high school. Now my sister's married to him. It's kind of crazy, really."

He made a sound that he hoped she took as agreement. He would call it a groan. "Crazy" pretty well described how she was making him feel.

"So, what about you?" she asked, again looking at him. "Do you like opera? Plays? The ballet?"

He knew she expected a negative answer. He wasn't sure he could even talk. "Depends."

Cocking her head, she frowned. "Are you all right? You sound funny."

He glanced down at his lap, where the nearness of her hand was arousing him. She also looked, and he knew the moment she understood the problem. Jerking back her hand, she began to scoot away. "I'm sorry. I didn't—"

He caught her wrist before she could escape. "Don't run off."

She tried to pull her fingers free from his grasp. "I didn't realize I was— I mean, I don't even like dogs."

Thor moved, getting up and padding across the room to another throw rug. Cody held on to Bernadette. "Now you've insulted him. Are you going to insult me, too, and tell me you don't like me?"

"I—" She hesitated. "Actually, I'm discovering you're a very nice person. It's just that—"

He understood. "We're too different."

"Totally."

"And every time I see you, I want to make love with you."

"And I—" She stared at him, shaking her head as his words registered. "No, you can't . . . We can't . . . It wouldn't work."

"Oh, I'm sure we could make love. Considering how you respond to a kiss, I think it would work very well."

"You know what I mean."

He knew. Just as he knew he needed to let go of her hand before he did something very foolish.

She rubbed her fingers over her wrist, but she didn't

Destiny Unknown

move. Slowly he reached forward, touching her cheek. She didn't look away, and he slid his fingers along the side of her face, cursing himself but unable to stop.

Skin as smooth and pale as polished beechnut, warm from the fire, met his touch. Wide-eyed, she watched him, her breathing shallow. As shallow as his.

"Kiss me," he whispered.

Bernadette knew she had to leave. She had to get away from him. Far, far away.

Tentatively she touched his chest. His shirt was soft, the linen giving beneath her fingertips. Leaning forward, she obeyed his command.

The blending of his mouth with hers was becoming a familiar experience, and she ran the tip of her tongue over his lips, catching the taste of chocolate. Chocolate was addicting. Cody was addicting.

His hands on her sides stabilized her, then she was falling, being carried with him to the thick rug. A twist and a turn, and he'd molded his body to hers, just as their lips were molded. Molded, yet moving.

Sensations spiraling through her took her breath away. Control was an illusion she couldn't hang on to, a delusion she shouldn't have trusted. That she liked what was happening scared her. The situation was all wrong.

The man was all wrong.

"Oh, Bernadette." He sighed her name close to her ear, the warmth of the words carrying her deeper into an abyss of pleasure.

Only a couple of hours before, another man's hands had touched her in much the same way that Cody was touching her. Yet nothing about Cody's touch was the same. She wanted to hold on to him, not escape. She wanted more, not less.

The molten need pouring through her begged for

relief, and his hips against hers were hard evidence that he shared her desire. Pins fell from her hair, and it flowed around her face, his fingers combing through it. The twisting and turning of their bodies had her dress to her hips, her legs free to wrap around his. Her nipples hardened, then radiated pleasure as his palms stroked across them.

She heard the groans and knew they were hers. Knew the sighs and the whimpering all came from a wanting she hadn't realized she possessed. A touch, ever so light between her legs, brought a gasp of delight. He leaned back, looking down at her.

His gaze was deep chocolate, tempting her. His voice was rough whiskey. "Either stop me now, or I'm going to make love with you."

SIX

"We have to stop." Bernadette hoped she'd said the words aloud. Her entire being was fighting the idea, urging her to go on. Physically, she wanted Cody. Emotionally, she needed protection. "I—I shouldn't have let things go this far."

His breathing erratic, Cody laughed at the irony. " 'Things' haven't gone far enough."

"You know what I mean."

"We both know."

Bernadette searched for the control she'd always had in the past. Finding it wasn't easy. *Leave,* her mind cried. *Leave before you're hurt, before he leaves you.*

How many years had she been doing that, protecting herself whenever she started to care?

Since Parker had left her?

Probably. Up until then, she'd still had hope that no matter how many times her father left, she wasn't the one at fault. Now being the first one to end a relationship was a way of life for her. Her sister even made jokes about it. And maybe Effie was right. Maybe she was always looking for a flaw in the men she dated. Why not find their flaws before they discovered hers?

Slowly she drew away. Cody said nothing, but his eyes held a plea. She looked to the side, afraid she might give in.

Normally she wouldn't object to the idea of making love. Not that she jumped into bed with every man who asked, but she wasn't a virgin and Cody wasn't a complete stranger. Normally she'd look at a night of lovemaking as a way to ease the tensions. With the right man, sex wasn't bad. It was one more aspect in a relationship that she could control.

Tonight, though, that wasn't true. Kissing Cody, lying with him in front of his fireplace, had been a volatile experience, explosive and uncontrollable. Kissing had led to wanting more, and she certainly wasn't relaxed. She rose to her feet, her entire body wound tight as a spring.

"Thank you for showing me around." She straightened her dress, barely glancing his way. He'd pushed himself up to a sitting position, and his gaze was on her, but he said nothing, his silence worse than words.

"And thanks for the hot chocolate." She'd barely touched hers, but she wasn't going to stay to finish it.

Her hand shaking, she reached for her purse. Cody's fingers touched hers, and the knot in her stomach tightened, her breath catching in her lungs.

"I'll walk you to your car," he said, and stood.

From the fireplace to the front door neither said a word. What more could be said? Bernadette wondered. She did thank him when he helped her on with her coat, and she repeated that she liked his "shack." Thor came out with them, trotting off on his own. At her car Cody opened her door, brushed a kiss across her forehead, and said good night. There were no more requests for her to

Destiny Unknown

stay, yet she knew he was asking. Even after her car door was closed and he stepped back, she saw the question in his eyes.

Bernadette drove off like a thief fleeing the scene of a crime, and for the rest of the weekend she kept waiting for Cody to show up. Her fear wasn't of him, but of what she might do. She'd said no, had asked him to stop, but could she do it again?

By Monday, Bernadette felt she had her life back under control. Cody hadn't called or come to see her, and she'd made a series of resolutions. First and foremost, she wouldn't see him again. Second, if by chance she did see him, she wouldn't kiss him. She knew enough not to play with fire. And third, she was going to start getting out more.

In Chicago she'd dated many men. Since moving to Grand Rapids, however, she hadn't had time. She hadn't thought it was a problem, but it was the only answer she could come up with as to why she was attracted to a man so clearly wrong for her.

Monday also gave her other things to think about. She had weekly reports from the department managers to review and a planning meeting to attend. Advertising copy had to be okayed, inventory and accounting sheets analyzed, and contractors called. Getting the renovations started was taking longer than she'd expected.

By midafternoon Morgan's Department Stores, not Cody Taylor, dominated her thoughts. That was, until Anne Closson knocked on her open door, a smile on her face. "You have a package."

Bernadette looked up from the papers on her desk. "A package?"

Still smiling, Anne entered Bern's office. "It arrived in an interesting way. Sherri in Cosmetics said she got it from her boyfriend, who got it from his boss, who said you left something at his place Friday night that he wanted to return."

Cody, Bernadette thought, but said nothing. Cautiously she took the package from Anne. The box was roughly the size of a shirt box, but as far as she knew, she hadn't left any clothing at Cody's. Her dress had stayed on, though just barely. Besides, whatever was in the box weighed more than a shirt or a dress.

She gave it a shake.

Anne stood where she was, watching. Bernadette shrugged. Shaking the box had given no clue to its contents, and she had no intention of opening the package in front of Anne. Maybe the woman was old enough to be her mother and had been a tremendous help in supplying information about the day-to-day management of Morgan's, but Bernadette wasn't about to tell her where she'd been Friday night . . . or what she'd done. She merely gave a nod. "Thank you."

A lift of her eyebrows expressed Anne's unspoken question, and she didn't move. Bern set the package on her desk. "I'll open it later."

She looked back down at the columns of figures in the report on her desk, trying to sound busy and distracted. "When you go out, could you close the door, please. I've got to get through these accounting figures before two."

"Certainly." Anne's formal tone of voice expressed her disappointment. She left, pulling the door closed behind her. As soon as Bernadette was sure it was safe, she reached for the package.

The crumpled newspapers inside the box had kept

Destiny Unknown

things from moving around. The paper surrounded a letter, the snapshot of her father that she'd shown Cody, and a box of Godiva chocolates.

I love Godiva chocolates, she remembered saying. He'd sent her some.

He'd sent her candy, returned her picture, and what else? A love letter?

Cautiously she unfolded the sheet of paper. Opened, the letter revealed a ticket to a ballet performance that was being held Friday night.

Bern frowned and read the letter, which had been written with a hurried scrawl.

She was still frowning when she crunched the paper into a ball and tossed it into her wastebasket. It seemed she wasn't the only one who'd done a lot of thinking over the weekend. She'd decided not to see him again. He'd decided to fly out to California to visit his sister's grave. It would be a quick visit, according to his note. He'd be back Friday. In time for the ballet. *See you there*, he'd written.

The man was out of his mind.

She stared at the single ticket and shook her head. Although she would love to see the performance, and the seat was excellent—orchestra, third row center—she certainly wasn't going to meet him there. Nor was she about to accept gifts from him, expecially a gift of candy.

The picture of her father went back into her purse, and she carried the ticket and box of chocolates out of her office. Anne was at her desk, and Loren was talking to her. Bernadette knew immediately what she was going to do. "I have something for each of you," she said as she approached the two. "You like chocolates, don't you?" She handed the box to Anne. "And how would you like a ticket to the ballet?" she asked Loren.

He cocked an eyebrow, and she smiled, picturing Cody's reaction Friday night. "It's only one ticket," she said. "There will be a man joining you." Her smile grew wider. "I met him last week, and I think you'll like him. You'll recognize him right away. He has brown hair, chestnut colored, that waves a little and hangs to his collar, and earrings—three of them. Hoops. And he always wears a gold chain around his neck. He's a bit unconventional."

"Unconventional?" Loren repeated, the eyebrow rising higher.

"That's what I said." She'd let him interpret the word any way he liked.

"And you were going to go out with him?"

"No." She shook her head, grinning. "He's not my type."

Friday night, as the hour neared eight, Bernadette wished she could see what was going on at DeVos Hall. What would happen when Loren sat down next to Cody? Loren wasn't shy, nor was he hesitant to let others know his sexual preferences.

Things could get interesting.

All evening Bernadette kept watching the clock. She made sure her lights were out and her door locked by ten-thirty, when she figured the ballet would be over. If Cody came by, he would think she was out or asleep. If he knocked, she wouldn't go to the door. When he called—and she was sure he would—she would tell him she didn't want to see him.

It was the only way to handle the situation. To be in the same room with him was too dangerous. He had a

Destiny Unknown

way of making her forget the tidy plans she'd made for her life.

Saturday morning Bern woke with an uneasy feeling. Cody hadn't called. It had been after midnight before she'd dropped off to sleep, and even then, it hadn't been a good, deep sleep. Every sound in her apartment had been magnified, every creak an imagined step in the hallway. Though her windows had been closed against the winter cold, she'd heard car doors opening and closing, and each time, her breath had caught in her throat as she'd waited for Cody to arrive at her door.

In a way, his absence was a disappointment. "Why can't you act like other men?" she grumbled, as she pulled on her coat.

Mopsy danced at her feet, and Bernadette grumbled again. She never should have promised to take care of her sister's dog for six weeks. Oh, Mopsy was cute, and it was nice to have a dog around at night, but Mopsy wanted to go out at the most inconvenient times. It wasn't even eight o'clock in the morning, but the way Mopsy was whining and prancing, Bernadette knew if she took time to put on her makeup or pull her hair back into a twist, she was going to be changing papers again. Of course, by her standards, she was going out half-dressed.

Her only consolation was that none of her neighbors ever got up this early on Saturdays, so there was little chance she'd run into anyone. A hat on her head and gloves on her hands, she took Mopsy out and waited in front of the apartment building as the dog sniffed one patch of grass after another. "Come on," she finally begged, the cold air getting to her. "For someone who had to get out here right away, you're taking long enough."

"She's picky . . . like someone else I know."

Bernadette cringed at the sound of the male voice. Without turning around, she knew Cody was behind her.

"Morning, Bern."

She faced him. "What are you doing here?"

He smiled, the wind blowing a strand of his hair across his face. It caught on the stubble of beard covering his jaw, and he pushed it aside. "Seems you're always asking me that."

"Because you keep popping up."

He was wearing the brown leather jacket he'd had on the first time she'd met him, jeans, and scuffed work boots. His hands were stuffed into the jacket's pockets, and his shoulders were hunched forward. If she hadn't known better, she would have taken him for a street person.

"Would you believe I was in the neighborhood?" he asked, his breath coming out as a steamy cloud.

"No." She had a feeling he'd been outside, waiting for her, for some time.

"I was stood up last night."

She shook her head. "You can only be stood up if you ask someone out, she says yes she'll go, and then doesn't show. You didn't ask; I didn't say yes."

A nod showed his appreciation of her logic. "I must say, I had an interesting evening, anyway."

She said nothing, though her curiosity begged for details.

He grinned. "Loren's an interesting person. We found we had a lot in common."

"Really." She lifted her eyebrows. "Did you show him your 'shack'?"

"We don't have *that much* in common." His chuckle was warm, not censuring. "What we have in common is he doesn't get along with his family either. Believe me, having just come back from visiting mine, it was nice to be able to talk to someone who understood."

"Glad things worked out well for you."

Her indifference irked Cody. Not that he would let her know. "Loren said he and his father disagree about everything: where Loren lives, his career choice, and his lifestyle. Sure sounded like my stepfather. Bill, of course, had his usual fit when he saw me. All week he was putting me down because of the earrings, the length of my hair, and my preference for jeans. You and he would probably get along great. Outward appearances are what count."

"Not necessarily what counts," she said, avoiding his gaze. "It's just . . . Well . . . I do think appearances are important."

Cody wasn't sure how that was different from what he'd said.

"What did Loren's father want him to be?" she asked.

A change of subject might be safer, Cody thought. "He wanted Loren to be a computer programmer. And I guess Loren tried it for a year before throwing in the towel."

"That explains why he knows so much about computers. You ought to see the Web page he's designing for Morgan's." She shook her head. "I'll tell you, I read the papers and know we need to use the Internet, that it's the wave of the future as far as sales and advertising go, but the idea of surfing the Net terrifies me. And when

Loren starts talking about computers, I'm totally lost. It took me a month just to figure out how to send e-mail to the other store."

Cody grinned. "He said you were cyberphobic. He also said you're doing a good job as general manager, much better than that Ben guy you replaced."

"Loren and Ben are always at each other's throats. Talk about opposites."

"Loren seems to feel that Ben causes more problems than he solves."

Bernadette frowned. "Did Loren say what kind of problems Ben is creating?"

Cody pointed at Mopsy, who'd finished her business. "He said Ben was the reason you and I met, that Ben brought the sponges into your office. He said he wouldn't be surprised if Ben had left the sponges and soup so Mopsy would get to them."

"You're saying Ben purposefully tried to hurt Mopsy?"

Cody wasn't sure. "I'm just saying what Loren told me, that he thinks Ben is jealous of you and would love to see you mess up. From what I heard the other day, I'd have to agree."

"I know it hasn't been easy for Ben, having me take his job, but to actually . . ."

She shook her head, and Cody noticed she was shivering. "Loren said some other things." He nodded toward her apartment building. "Why don't we go inside, where it's warmer, and I'll tell you everything. Had your breakfast yet?"

"No, I don't—"

He didn't give her a chance to finish. "Good. I make a mean omelette." A whistle caught Mopsy's attention. "Come on, puppy dog." With a hand at Bernadette's

Destiny Unknown

back, he guided her toward her apartment. "You'll get a kick out of some of the things Loren said."

She resisted against his hand. "Wait. I . . . We—"

Cody dropped his hand from her back. She was going to come up with her usual arguments, all perfectly logical and reasonable. Problem was, his feelings for her weren't logical, and he'd already listened to his own arguments as to why he shouldn't see her again. Since he hadn't heeded his own counsel, why should he heed hers?

Keeping his expression serious, he walked ahead, following Mopsy. He knew what would silence her. "By the way, what are you doing about the shoplifting ring that's been hitting your store?"

"Shoplifting ring?" Bernadette hurried to catch up.

Bernadette wasn't exactly sure how Cody had ended up in her kitchen, an apron covering the front of his jeans and the sleeves of his sweater shoved up to his elbows. One minute they were talking about shoplifters, the next he was hanging his jacket in her closet and getting eggs out of her refrigerator.

"So, Loren isn't really sure there's a shoplifting ring," she said, summarizing what Cody had said.

"He has no solid proof, if that's what you mean, just what one of his assistants told him he saw. But if Loren's right, I'd say these people are pros. From the assistant's account, one guy was doing a good job of distracting your salesclerk while two women were taking merchandise right off the counter."

"But what about the surveillance detectors we have in place? They should pick up any merchandise being taken out of the store that hasn't been cleared at the register."

"Oh, come on. I may not be in the retail business, but I'll bet those detectors are easy to get around if you know what to do. And didn't you say you were having problems with them?"

"Yes." She nursed the cup of coffee Cody had given her, mulling over his words. A ring of shoplifters would explain the rise in losses off the floor. What she hated to consider was Cody's last statement. If the detectors weren't being accidentally triggered to go off, then someone inside the store was involved. Disturbed, she looked up. "Why hasn't Loren reported this to me?"

Cody turned away from the stove to face her. "Loren said he did report it to Ben, and Ben said he would handle it. Except, yesterday, when Loren asked Ben what he was doing, Ben didn't give him a straight answer."

"Ben never gives you a straight answer." Straight answers required decision making, which Ben couldn't handle. She sighed, not quite sure how to handle the situation herself. "I wish Loren had come to me first."

"I'm not sure he felt he could."

Cody went back to his cooking. Bernadette frowned at his back. "Why not?"

"Oh, come on, Bern. You can be intimidating."

Cody scooped half an omelette each onto two plates, grabbed the English muffins that he'd already toasted and buttered, and carried the food to the table. She watched him, his statement playing through her mind. "How am I intimidating?"

"How?" He set one plate in front of her, placed the muffins in the middle of the table, and sat across from her. "Princess, let's face it, you don't give out a lot of

Destiny Unknown

warm fuzzies that invite people to get close. There's a wall around you that keeps others away. It's in your posture, your self-control, your clothes—" His glance dropped to her clothes. "Well, maybe not this morning, but usually."

Bernadette also looked down at her clothes. Thanks to Mopsy's desperate need to get outside, all she'd taken time to put on were a pair of gray wool slacks, ankle-high leather boots, and a thick cable-knit sweater. With the sweater, she hoped its rich coral color made up for her lack of makeup and that it was heavy enough to disguise the absence of a bra.

"My posture and clothes certainly didn't intimidate you that first time we met," she reminded him. "Talk about getting close. You were leaning up against me, rubbing elbows."

He grinned. "Not because of any invitation on your part. In fact, the way you looked at me and acted screamed 'Stay away.' I got close because I liked seeing you squirm."

"You're not only irritating, you admit it."

"At least I'm honest about it. Every time I meet you, the messages I get are 'Don't touch, don't get under my skin. Don't find out if I have weaknesses.'"

She sent him a leveling glare. "Then why not heed those messages?"

"Ah, that's the rub." He grinned. "I also get another message, one that says you are interested."

"Well, you're wrong about that message."

"Am I?" he asked, his voice soft and gentle. "Why do you make it so difficult to get close, Bernadette?"

"Why waste our time?"

"Maybe it wouldn't be a waste."

She looked down at her eggs, bothered by the intensity of his gaze. "This conversation is ridiculous. And if you think you're going to talk me into going out with you, you're wrong."

"I suppose we could skip the going out and go straight to bed."

The suggestion should have been insulting. She shouldn't be feeling a tightening in her body or a surge of anticipation. Shouldn't feel her pulse rate increase. She opened her mouth to retort, but no words came out.

He smiled and motioned toward her plate with his fork. "Try your eggs."

Try her eggs? She stabbed at the omelette on her plate. What she'd like to try was a stab at Cody. He didn't act like men she knew and didn't react as she expected. He showed up when he shouldn't. Didn't show up when he should. He was impossible.

She chewed a bite of eggs and came to one more conclusion. He made a hell of an omelette.

"Not bad," she mumbled.

"Thank you. Oh, and you missed a good performance last night. They did scenes from Tchaikovsky's *Swan Lake*, *The Sleeping Beauty*, and *The Nutcracker Suite*."

"I was busy," she lied, and reached for an English muffin.

He reached for one at the same time. Their hands touched, and she jerked hers back. He smiled, picked up a muffin and placed it on her plate, then got one for himself.

"Weather was great in California," he said, going on as if they always had breakfast together. "Not hot, but in the high sixties. Flowers everywhere. What a shock to come back to Michigan. Here we are into March, and they're still predicting snow."

"Maybe you should move back to California. North of your stepfather's house, of course."

Cody grinned. "It would fit the fairy tale, but I like it here in Michigan. Too many people in California, most of them a little crazy."

She laughed. "And you're not?"

"Perfectly sane," he said, though he had some doubts this morning. He'd just spent an hour in freezing temperatures waiting for a woman who didn't want to see him. "Speaking of crazy, I get my truck back Monday. You heard from that nut at all?"

"He called and apologized. Blamed what he did on the alcohol. Then he asked me out."

"And?"

She lifted neatly shaped eyebrows. "Do you really think I would go out with him after what he did?"

"I hope not."

"I'm not stupid."

"No." He was, though, Cody thought. She'd walked away from him three times. Only an idiot would keep trying.

Finishing his eggs, he stood up. "Hate to eat and run, but I've got things to do."

She looked up at him, confusion drawing her brows together. "You're leaving?"

"Gotta. Just wanted to stop by and say hi and let you know you missed a good performance."

She pushed her chair back, dabbed at her mouth with her napkin, and stood. "I didn't thank you for returning that picture of my father. Oh, and thank you for the chocolates."

Cody started for the door. "Did you enjoy them?"

The look in her eyes said it all. He shook his head. "You didn't eat them, did you?"

"I, ah—I've been trying to watch my weight."

"You gave away the chocolates and you gave away the ticket." Her message was loud and clear.

"I, ah—"

"That's okay." He waved off her excuses. If she didn't want him around, he wasn't about to fight it. She might be beautiful, but beauty was only skin deep. She might have problems, but so what? Dumb John wasn't going to solve this princess's problems.

SEVEN

Bernadette watched Cody stride off. Even after he'd left the building, she stood in her doorway, not quite sure what to think. Once again he'd popped into her life, had stirred up emotions she didn't want stirred, then had left. How could he tease her like that? Leave her, just as her father always left her?

"Damn him!" She quelled an urge to pound the door with her fist. She would not lose control. She would not let him get to her.

Except he already had.

"What are you doing to me?" She closed her eyes, thinking back over everything Cody had said and done that morning.

She didn't know how long he'd been out in the cold, waiting for her. Hearing his voice and seeing him had triggered strange sensations in her body. "I suppose we could go straight to bed," he'd said.

Maybe that's what they should do. Maybe if they made love, had sex and got it over with, she could get him out of her system. It didn't have to mean anything.

It wouldn't mean anything. How could it? They were totally wrong for each other.

Walking back to the kitchen, Bernadette smiled. The idea of making love with Cody seemed a bit anticlimactic. He'd just walked out on her. One minute they were having breakfast together, the next he was gone.

She pushed open the kitchen door and stared at the table. Mopsy had gotten up on her chair and was licking the last of the omelette off Bernadette's plate.

Not only was Cody gone, so was her breakfast.

Tuesday, Bernadette wondered why she'd ever left Chicago. She'd never had the problems there that she was having now. The EAS systems were still giving her fits, first one surveillance unit malfunctioning downtown, then one at the Twenty-eighth Street store. If someone was causing the problems, she didn't have the foggiest idea how.

No more than she understood why a shipment of spring dresses that should have been delivered that week had been canceled, or why the supplier was swearing she was the one who'd canceled the order. It didn't make sense. She wouldn't have canceled that order.

Nor would she have approved the ad that had run in Sunday's paper with all the wrong prices. Yet the advertising department of the Grand Rapids' *Press* was swearing the ad was printed exactly as okayed. They'd even shown her the approved artwork—with her signature.

She couldn't have okayed those prices.

Wouldn't have.

Yet it was her signature in the corner. She held a copy of the page in her hand.

Whatever was going on, she didn't like it. Shipping

Destiny Unknown

and Receiving was upset. Security was upset. The entire sales force was upset. And the last time she'd seen Ben, he'd had a smirk on his face that almost yelled, "You're out of here."

Which she would be if Parker showed up anytime soon. Sister-in-law or not, he would can her, and she wouldn't blame him. He'd hired her to make things easier for him, not to ruin his business.

A headache throbbed in her temple, and she spoke to no one on her way back to her office. What she needed was some time alone, time to think. "Hold my calls," she said as she walked past Anne's desk.

"He's in there," Anne answered, pointing toward Bernadette's closed office door.

Bern stopped before opening the door. "He?" She frowned. "Parker?"

Anne shook her head and smiled knowingly. "He. Him. The one who took you to lunch a couple weeks ago. Mr. Godiva-chocolates-and-a-ticket-to-the-ballet."

"Cody?" Bern stared at the door. She didn't have the energy to face Cody. Not today. Not now.

"I wasn't going to let him in," Anne said. "But Loren came by and said it would be all right, that you and Mr. Good-Looking are—" She paused dramatically. "Friends."

"Acquaintances," Bern said, though she knew they were more than that. More than acquaintances and less than friends. Certainly less than lovers, and the way Anne was smiling, it was clear she thought they were lovers. "I barely know him."

Anne nodded, still smiling.

"The guy wears earrings and a gold chain."

"And has absolutely gorgeous eyes."

Bernadette had to agree. She looked back at her door. "What does he want?"

"Why don't you go in and find out?"

She supposed she had to. It was her office. Though when she opened the door, Bernadette wondered about that. Cody was leaning back in her chair as if he owned the place, his boots propped up on her desk, her telephone to his ear. He smiled when he saw her and waved. "I'll be just a minute," he mouthed.

Bernadette carefully shut her door, then exploded. "Get off my phone! And get your feet off my desk."

He dropped his feet to the floor, and sat up straight. Watching her, he spoke into the phone. "I'll have to call you later, Jack. We can discuss this then."

The phone went back into its cradle, and he stood as Bernadette walked toward her desk. This was no enchanted princess in need of his help, he thought. Neatly dressed in a tailored black suit, not a blond hair out of place and her gold jewelry perfectly coordinated, Bernadette was the image of sophistication and elegance, a woman in control. It was her eyes that told more, her anger sparking hot blue.

"You invade my office," she said, her voice not quite level. "Take over my desk. Make phone calls. Act like you own the place—"

She stopped on the opposite side of her desk. The breath she drew in was shaky, the lines of her mouth tight. He gave no excuses, but moved to her side. "I need to talk to you about something."

"Well I don't want to talk to you . . . about anything."

She was as bristly as a porcupine. He countered with a smile. "Rough day or PMS?"

The moment he said it, he knew he'd made a mistake. Her glare turned to pure ice. "Why is it you men always want to blame everything on PMS? For decades you didn't believe women even had anything like that, now it's the explanation for all behavior that doesn't suit your fancy."

"Rough day, I take it."

She drew in a breath, turned away, and walked around to her chair. Only when she was seated, her desk again between them, did she look his way. "It's been a hell of a day, so whatever you have to say, make it fast. I don't have time for chitchat or games."

"This is no game." And what he had to say wasn't going to make her day any better, but Cody knew he couldn't help that. Either the lady was a thief or she needed his help. Needed it desperately. "I was over at True Fidelity today, talking to Frank Pierce about my new development. Your name came up, and he asked me a rather disturbing question."

"Which was?" Her posture was rigid, her tone suspicious.

Cody didn't answer. Pulling up one of the two leather chairs in front of her desk, he settled himself into a comfortable position. Maybe a little game playing wasn't a bad idea, a little stalling. "You look tired," he said.

"I'm not tired. I have a headache." She rubbed her fingertips over her right temple, and her shoulders drooped a little. The lapse in her defensive attitude lasted only a moment, then her hand dropped back to the desktop, and she glared at him. "But that's beside the point. What was this question Frank asked that disturbed you so much you had to invade my office?"

"Taken anything for it . . . your headache, that is?"

"No, and—"

From his jacket pocket he pulled a bottle of aspirins and tossed it onto her desk. She looked down at the bottle, then back at him.

"I always carry some with me," he said. "Take a couple."

She picked up the bottle, but didn't open it. "Are you going to tell me this question Frank asked, or do I have to call him to find out?"

It seemed he couldn't put it off any longer. "Actually, there were two questions Frank asked. First he wanted to know how well I knew you. Then he wanted to know if I trusted you."

"If you trusted me?"

"He's concerned." Cody decided to simply ask. "What he'd like to know—I guess what we'd both like to know—is why you opened a personal account at True Fidelity the day after Parker left on his honeymoon."

"What personal account?" Her frown brought the carefully sculpted lines of her blond brows together.

"The account that's being fed into on a daily basis from Morgan's Department Stores."

She sat forward, the rigid control slipping. "You're out of your mind."

"Am I?" He hoped she had a better explanation than that.

"I have a personal savings and checking account at the First of America Bank here in town, but nothing at True Fidelity, though Frank has hinted that I should switch my money over to his bank."

"His records show that you opened an account on the third Monday in February. The next day, money was electronically deposited into that account. Not a lot of money. I think it was thirty dollars the first day."

"I didn't put thirty dollars in any account."

Destiny Unknown

"Not you. The transfer came directly from Morgan's. Since then, deposits have been made on a daily basis. Never huge amounts. Twenty, thirty dollars at a time. All transfers. All coming from Morgan's."

Cody knew when she understood what he was suggesting. Her eyes widened, her mouth opened slightly. "And you think I—? Frank thinks—?" She closed her eyes, shaking her head. "Either you two are crazy, or I am."

"Well, I know I'm not crazy. And I don't think you are."

She took in a breath, and looked at him again. The fire was gone from her eyes, replaced by clouds of concern. "Then you tell me why I would open an account at a bank and not remember it. Why I would okay an ad for the *Press* that had all the wrong prices. Give me one good reason why I would cancel an order for dresses we desperately need on the racks. I'll even bet Frank has my signature on something authorizing the account at his bank."

"He said he has." Cody had asked if Bernadette had actually come to the bank to open the account. Frank had said no, but he had all the paperwork and her signature card on file.

Frank had really gone beyond proper business ethics by telling Cody about the account. Friendship had initiated the conversation: Frank's friendship with him and with Parker. Frank had asked how well he knew Bernadette, then had wondered aloud if Parker really knew his sister-in-law. Cody had taken it from there, coercing more information from Frank. Now he needed more information from Bernadette. "Explain the connection between your opening an account at True Fidelity and a dress order and an ad."

"No connection that I'm aware of, other than my signature seems to be appearing all over the place, and people keep telling me I've done things I know I haven't."

She handed him a folded piece of paper, and Cody quickly opened it and scanned the page. It was a copy of the artwork for Morgan's weekly ad, and in the lower right corner was a date and Bernadette Sanders's signature okaying the ad.

"I didn't sign that," she said. "I signed advertising copy for last Sunday's ad, but it wasn't this copy. I would never approve an ad with those prices."

"But this is your signature?"

"It's mine, or a damned good forgery. And the signature's not a Xerox copy. The original, the one on file at the *Press*, is in blue ink. And in California I have a supplier who swears I sent a cancellation form to him on an order that was supposed to be delivered last week. He says he has the form with my signature. He's sending me a copy. Again, he says the signature is in blue ink while the rest is typed."

"And you usually use a blue pen when you sign something?"

"Not always, but usually, yes."

"So suddenly you have orders canceled, ads running with the wrong prices, and—"

"A bank account I didn't open." Once again she frowned. "I'm not skimming Parker. I wouldn't do that, even if he weren't my brother-in-law."

"Well, someone's certainly trying to make it look as if you are."

"But why?" She closed her eyes, her shoulders sagging and her head drooping. "Why is any of this happening?"

Destiny Unknown

Suddenly her eyes snapped open, and her chin came back up. "Ben?"

Cody considered the idea. "You took his job. He might think he could discredit you, make you look bad, and get his job back. I'd say it was a real possibility."

"But how is he doing it?"

That was the question they needed to answer. Cody handed back the ad copy. "Does Ben have you sign things? Orders? Forms? Anything where he could slip something else in that you might sign without knowing?"

She shook her head. "I always read everything I sign."

"You never get in a rush?"

Bernadette started to say no, then stopped herself. Normally she didn't get in a rush, but with Parker gone, nothing had been normal. "Maybe once in a while."

"So Ben could sneak something through 'once in a while'?"

Once again she picked up the bottle of aspirins on her desk. This time she opened it and shook two into the palm of her hand. She didn't want to think Ben would do such a thing. They'd had their differences, but she liked the man. He—

Cody rose to his feet, and she stopped her thoughts to watch him walk to her office door. He'd popped back into her life, had basically accused her of being a thief, then had suggested she was being framed by someone. Now it looked like he was leaving.

She wasn't sure why she was surprised. That's what her father always did—showed up for a while, played the hero, then took off. No explanations given. No warnings.

Cody opened the door and called, "Anne, could you get Ms. Sanders a glass of water, please?"

The moment Cody started back to his chair, Bernadette looked away. She didn't want him to see her relief. She didn't want him to think she gave a damn if he stayed or left. "Thank you," she mumbled, and set the aspirins aside to wait for the water.

She was in control again by the time he sat down. "I'll call Frank," she said. "Have him close that account."

Cody shook his head. "I'd call him, if I were you, but don't close the account. Explain what's going on and have him monitor things from his end, then alert the authorities. Don't bring them here. You go to them. Around here, don't let on that you even know about the account. Don't talk to Ben or anyone about it. The less you seem to know, the better your chances are of finding out something."

"Finding out something, or running Parker out of business?" She once again held up the ad page. "This cost the stores money. Not having merchandise on hand costs us money. Every time I turn around, something is happening that equals a financial loss for Morgan's."

From a folder on her desk, she pulled another sheet of paper. "This is a note from one of our security guards. I followed up on what you said Saturday, on what Loren told you. First I asked several of our senior associates if they'd seen anything suspicious, any signs of shoplifting. Two said they've seen a man and two women who have aroused their suspicions. So I alerted Security, and found this on my desk this morning."

She handed Cody the paper, but went on to summarize what it said. "Carl is the guard on duty during the day. He thinks we're being hit here, and that the trio's

Destiny Unknown

targeting departments where the clerks aren't very attentive. Of course, if we're being hit here, we're probably being hit at the Twenty-eighth Street store too. And if these shoplifters know which clerks are inattentive, they know the stores well . . . know our personnel."

Cody glanced over the note, then back at her. "Have you had any more problems with the electronic surveillance system?"

"Every day. They're driving us crazy. I'm ready to pull all of them and get a new system."

There was a sharp rap on her door, and Bernadette called, "Come in."

Anne entered with a paper cup of water. She smiled at Cody, and Bernadette suppressed a smile of her own. The guy was a lady-killer, that's what he was. Young and old, they fell at his feet.

As soon as she had the water, Bern swallowed the aspirins, but she waited until Anne had left the room before pursuing the conversation. "At least it's nice to know I'm not going out of my mind."

"It's nice for me to know you're not a thief."

"So you did think I was." Disappointment cut through her.

"If I really thought you were, I wouldn't have come here to see you."

"I could be lying."

"You could be, but I don't think you are."

"You barely know me. What's it been? Two weeks since we met?"

"Two weeks and a day." He grinned. "I'd like to know you better, but you keep pushing me away."

She thought back to their last encounter. "You're the one who walked away Saturday morning."

Pensively he sat back in his chair, his elbows on the

arms, his hands steepled in front of him. A wry smile quirked his mouth. "And I wasn't coming back, Princess. What do you think? Are we fated to be together?"

"Maybe ill-fated." As ill-fated as all of her relationships with men turned out to be.

"I certainly hope not."

The soft way he said the words, and the intensity of his gaze, disturbed her. She shifted positions in her chair. "So, what's next?"

His grin turned wicked. "We could go to my place and make love for the rest of the afternoon."

The idea of making love with Cody turned her stomach inside out. Hadn't she had a similar thought just three days ago? How easy it had been to rationalize the idea of sleeping with him after he'd walked out on her. Now staring across her desk at him, seeing him, as they said, in the flesh, she knew she wasn't ready—never would be ready—to make love with Cody Taylor. The idea was simply too scary. "That wasn't what I meant."

"I know." He rose to his feet and started around her desk toward her.

She watched him every step of the way, the knot in her stomach tightening. "What are you doing?"

"You asked what's next." He slipped behind her. "What I think we need is to look at this from a different angle."

His hands touched her shoulders, his fingers gliding to her neck, and she twisted her head to look up at him. "I don't understand. What—?"

"Am I doing now?" he finished for her, all the while moving his fingertips in small circles over the nape of her neck. "One of best the ways I've found to come up with new ideas is to do something totally unrelated to what I'm thinking about. So, my dear princess, I'm going to give you a massage. It may also help that headache of yours."

"I don't need a massage." What she needed was a reality check. Just the touch of his hands had her on edge; a tingly sensation ran down her spine.

"Put your head forward."

"This is a crazy idea. I don't have time for—"

A slight nudge from his hand pushed her head forward, and her protest dissolved under the gentle rubbing of his fingers. In spite of herself she groaned in pleasure, tucking her chin tighter to her chest and giving him better access to her neck and shoulders. She might not need a massage, but it certainly felt good. Closing her eyes, she chuckled. "Dang you, Cody. You are so exasperating. Don't you ever listen to what someone tells you?"

"Not when I know it's not true. Your neck is all tied up in knots."

He should see her stomach.

"Relax," he ordered.

How could she when the rough warmth of his callused fingers was creating an awareness deep within her, teasing her into wanting more? He was seducing her in subtle ways, vanquishing one tension to create another. Only ten minutes earlier her thoughts had been focused on the myriad problems facing her. Now nothing seemed important, nothing but absorbing the warmth and strength of Cody's hands and melting into the oblivion of sensory overload.

His leather jacket scrunched against the back of her chair like soft butter, releasing its heady scent. She licked her lips and tasted the wanting his nearness triggered. His voice, when he spoke, was like a caress. "I know this isn't a fairy tale, Princess. But you do have problems, and I would like to help you."

The idea of Cody helping her was ironic. She needed to be saved from him, rescued from the emotional turmoil he created in her. Valiantly she struggled to regain control of her dazed thoughts. "You have helped," she said shakily. "When I came into this office a few minutes ago, I couldn't figure out what was going on. I thought I was losing my mind. Now everything makes sense. The irrational has become rational."

But the way she reacted to Cody wasn't rational. How easy it would be to give in to his suggestion to make love. How desperately she wanted to.

"You're still tense," he said, and she laughed. She was more than tense.

He tilted her head back and worked his fingertips up along the line of her jaw to her temples. "I don't know why I thought I could stay away from you," he said, his voice huskier than just a moment before.

Bernadette watched his mouth move. Funny how a person looked completely different when viewed from below. She could see the stubble of Cody's beard under his chin and along his jawline. His nose was slightly flared, his eyes veiled by thick brown lashes. The total picture was somewhat ghoulish, and she knew what she was seeing was his other side, just as he would one day see her other side. Now he was attracted to her, but the day would come when he would leave for good.

"No." She pulled away from his touch, straightening in her chair. Her heart pounding in her chest, she didn't dare look at him. "I told you from the beginning, I'm not interested in starting anything with you."

"So you did," he said, his tone suddenly very cool.

Destiny Unknown

"Several times, in fact. And you're right, I don't listen, but I should."

Not until he stepped away from her desk and started for the door did she realize she'd been holding her breath. For a moment she simply watched, knowing she'd never see him again, then she rose to her feet and followed. "Thanks for coming and telling me what Frank said. At least I now know what's going on."

Cody paused before opening her door. "I think Parker also needs to know what's going on."

She disagreed. "Not while he's on his honeymoon. My sister set it up so he'll have six weeks completely away from these stores. I'm the general manager. I'm the one who needs to resolve this; otherwise, he might as well fire me."

"Someone wants you to fail."

"At least in this case, if I do fail, I'll know why."

Cody frowned at her answer. "I don't want you getting hurt."

She saw the concern in his eyes and believed him. "It won't be the first time. I've just got to stay in control."

He stared at her, saying nothing, then he swore, and his hands—those big, rough, callused hands—cradled her face, and she knew he was going to kiss her.

EIGHT

Bernadette had come to expect the unexpected from Cody, yet she wasn't ready for this assault on her senses. From the touch of his hands to the taste of his mouth, he wiped out the last bit of sanity she possessed. She held on to him like a wanton woman, kissing him back. In that one act, her protests that she wasn't interested were exposed as blatant lies. He would indeed have to be dumb not to see. The truth was, she wanted him more than she'd ever wanted a man.

And he wanted her. With her body pressed against his, she knew he was fully aroused. The idea of making love was becoming more of a need than a fantasy.

He was the one who pulled them back to reality. "Wow," he said, a rough edge to his voice. "I, ah—"

She watched him struggle for control, his eyes dark with passion and his breathing uneven. She was dealing with her own struggles, afraid to admit what they both knew.

He didn't push. Stepping back, he gave them both time to regroup. Only when she started to say something

Destiny Unknown

did he act. With a finger to her lips and a shake of his head, he stopped her protest. "I'm leaving now. I'll call you later."

She knew he would.

He glanced around her office, then walked over and picked up one of the color sample books a contractor had left. "Do you need this today?"

Unsure why he wanted it, she shook her head.

"Good. I'll get it back to you." He grinned, casually positioning the book so it covered the front of his jeans. "Certain disadvantages to tight jeans."

As she stood in her doorway, watching him stride out of the office area, she knew she'd lost complete control of the situation. William Cody Taylor hadn't popped into her life, he'd barged in.

"Just an acquaintance, huh?" Anne said, and a rush of heat flowed to Bernadette's cheeks. Anne was no more than two feet away, her grin knowing.

"We, ah—" Bernadette groped for an explanation. "That is—"

"Loren said he's in construction."

Cody had evidently given Loren the same spiel he'd given her when they first met. Bernadette didn't want Anne thinking Cody was just a construction worker. "He built Parker's apartment building."

Anne watched Cody turn the corner in the hallway and disappear. "That's the guy? He drove Parker nuts."

"He seems to have that effect on a lot of people." He was certainly driving her crazy. He'd also brought her information she needed to act on. It was time to find out what was going on. "Anne, do you remember if I sent anything over to Frank Pierce at True Fidelity a couple of weeks ago?"

"True Fidelity?" Anne repeated, her attention coming back to Bernadette.

"I just found out—" Bernadette stopped herself. She trusted Anne, but Anne's allegiance was to Parker, Ben, and Loren. Bernadette was the newcomer, and though she and Anne had a good working relationship, Bern wasn't a hundred percent sure Anne would believe her over Ben.

"I just found out," she began again, "that Frank thinks I'm going to—to be at a function Friday night that True Fidelity is putting on. I sure can't remember sending him anything saying I could go, and I can't make it."

Anne started for her desk. "You want me to call and tell him?"

"No . . . no, I'll do that."

Pausing, Anne turned back. "What did you find out about the ad in the *Press*?"

"It's definitely my signature on the ad." Bernadette wasn't sure if she should ask, then knew she had to. "Do you think Ben would slip something like that past me, get me to sign a messed-up ad so I'd look bad in Parker's eyes?"

"Ben?" Anne frowned. "No. Sure, he was hurt when Parker brought you in, but he's too nice a guy to do something like that."

Bernadette wondered.

She went home late, fed Mopsy and took the dog for a walk, then heated a bowl of soup for herself. As she ate she jotted down all of the incidents that had occurred since Parker had left. Her conversations with Frank and the police that afternoon had left her unsettled. Frank had seemed as friendly as usual, but she'd noticed a cautiousness and a lack of warmth in his voice, especially when she repeated Cody's suggestion that the account not be closed.

With the police, she wasn't sure the officer she'd spoken with even took her seriously. He'd asked her to repeat her story three times, and when she'd said her signature was appearing on documents she knew she hadn't signed, he'd chuckled and said his wife was always using that excuse. What had really blown her top was when she'd said everything had started after Parker left, and the officer's comment had been, "All goes to hell when the man goes away." She'd accused him of chauvinism and had threatened to go to his superior. That had brought an apology, but Bernadette had returned to the downtown store feeling uneasy. At this point it was her word against Ben's, and it was her signature on everything. She had to figure out how Ben was doing it.

She jumped when her telephone rang. A glance at her clock showed it was after eight. She answered on the second ring. It was Ben.

"Did you get the e-mail from Parker?" he asked.

"What e-mail?"

"It's addressed to you, Anne, Loren, and me. It's from Australia." Ben chuckled. "When your sister said she was getting him far, far away from here, she wasn't kidding."

"Effie didn't want him finding excuses to check on how things were going. I'm surprised she let him send an e-mail."

"It's not very long. There are a couple lines in the message from her to you. Aren't you checking your e-mail?"

Bernadette caught the accusation. "I didn't have time

today." She'd had other things on her mind. Bank accounts she hadn't opened and signatures that were but weren't hers. "So, what did Parker and Effie have to say?"

"That they're having a good time, are staying at a place where the guests can send e-mail messages to friends and relatives, and they'll be there until tomorrow morning, so if we wanted to get a message to them, we could. Do you want me to tell him about the problems we've been having here?"

She could almost hear the laughter in Ben's voice and could imagine the smirk on his face. She kept her tone level. "No, why worry him? The man's on his honeymoon. I'm sure we'll have this figured out by the time he gets back."

"Whatever you say, boss."

The smirk was definitely there, irking her, and she couldn't resist saying more. "I feel I'm getting closer to an answer all the time."

That, she hoped, would give him something to worry about. Ben's response, however, indicated no concern on his part. "Sounds good to me," he said. "I'll e-mail him back that all is fine."

Bernadette wished there was a way she could get into Ben's computer and see what he actually did send to Parker. Computers, however, were not her forte. When Parker had first showed her the setup they had, he'd asked if she would have any problems. He didn't know that much about computers himself, but he saw the marketing potential inherent in the Internet. She'd said that what she didn't know, she would learn. And she had been learning.

Anne had helped, as well as Loren and Ben. They all used their computers on a regular basis, sending e-mail

Destiny Unknown

messages between the downtown store and the Twenty-eighth Street store and browsing the Internet for information regarding retailing trends. Loren was the one who'd suggested a Web page for Morgan's. She had helped there. She might not know how to get on and browse the Internet, but she knew a Web site was the right direction to be moving in and had supported Loren. And Loren's initial setup pages were beautiful. It was only when he started explaining how he was doing it that she had no idea what he was talking about. A call to him might clue her in on how to find out what Ben had sent, but she doubted even Loren knew Ben's password. Her best bet might be to go in and send something to Parker herself.

She was slipping on her coat when the telephone rang again. She thought it might be Ben calling back.

It was Cody.

"Hi," he said, the whiskey-smooth timbre of his voice sending a shiver down her spine. "I said I'd call, but I forgot I had a meeting. This is the first chance I've had to get away. How did things go this afternoon?"

She leaned against the wall, closing her eyes and remembering her meetings with Frank and the police. "I survived."

"You talked to Frank?"

"I did." She heard voices in the background at the other end of the line. She had no idea where Cody was, but he wasn't alone. She kept her answer brief. "I'm not sure I convinced him I didn't know anything about that account. I think I should have closed it."

"Closed, you find out nothing. Open, you may be able to trace who set it up and how."

"I hope you're right. Ben called me tonight."

"What did he want?"

"Seems Parker sent a group e-mail message to the store asking how things are going. I was so busy this afternoon, I never turned on my computer, so I didn't see it. Ben wanted to know if he should tell Parker about the problems we've been having."

"And you said?"

"I told him no, but I'm going in right now to send my own e-mail message to Parker, just in case Ben decided to stir the pot a little."

"I thought you said Ben had trouble making decisions."

"I'm beginning to wonder if we've all underestimated Ben's decision-making abilities."

Bernadette arrived at the store before nine o'clock, turned on her computer, and read the message from Parker. It was basically what Ben had said, a quick summary of where they were, how they'd managed to get on-line, and when they would be leaving. Effie's addition was a quick hi and a warning that even if the roof was falling down around everyone's heads, Parker wasn't coming back for another four weeks. Bernadette hoped four weeks would be enough time to figure out what was going on. She hit the Reply button and typed in a quick, reassuring message that everything was under control. Once it was sent, she logged off and leaned back in her chair.

Outside her door she could hear the last of the staff leaving. Morgan's was closed for the night, the building deserted except for the cleaning staff and nighttime security guard. Considering how little she'd accomplished that day and how much work was piled on her desk, she

Destiny Unknown

decided to stay. She could accomplish a lot in an hour without any interruptions.

More than two hours later Bernadette stretched and glanced at her watch. It was nearly midnight. She slipped on her coat, picked up her purse, and quietly exited her office.

The two women cleaning the office area looked up at her. "You still working?" one asked with a slight accent. "Is late."

"Very late." Bernadette suppressed a yawn. "But I got a lot accomplished. Maybe I'll have to start coming in at night."

The other cleaning woman shook her head. "You and Mr. Waite."

"What about Mr. Waite?" Bernadette perked up at the mention of Ben's name.

"Many times he work until way after midnight."

It wasn't much, Bernadette knew, but it might mean something. "Is he here tonight?"

The two cleaning ladies looked at each other. Each shrugged and the second one spoke. "If so, we didn't see him. Was he supposed to be?"

"No. I was just curious. Have a nice night."

Bernadette left the office area and headed for the escalator. The store was only dimly lit, a strange silence pervading the building. Gone were the salesclerks and customers, the sound of cash registers ringing up sales, and the music that always played in the background. Now the sound of her heels clicking on the tiles carried from display area to display area, and the mannequins she passed took on an eerie life of their own.

A fear of the dark wasn't one of her weaknesses, yet

Bernadette felt a kick of adrenaline speed up her heart. Each step she took down the stilled escalator took her deeper into the silence, and she found herself hesitating before she reached the bottom. Quickly she scanned what she could see of the first-floor sales area. The security guard should be around somewhere.

All was still.

The glow of a light in the Shipping and Receiving area caught her attention. Ben's office was there, as well as Loren's. According to Parker, when Ben was hired as general manager, he'd asked for the office down there rather than the one Bernadette now occupied. He'd said he would have a better feel for the store there. She preferred being on the second floor, but at least she hadn't had to kick Ben out of his office when she took over his position.

Her car was parked across the street in the garage of the Amway Hotel, and the closest exit was through the front doors, but if she went out the side door, she would pass Ben's office and could see if he was there, or if it was simply the cleaning staff or the security guard who had the light on.

The first two steps she took off the escalator clicked loudly through the empty store. Rising up on her toes, she silenced the sound. At the same time, the light in the office went out. Bernadette stopped and waited, the thudding of her heart reverberating in her ears. It could be a coincidence, or it could be someone didn't want to be seen.

She thought she heard a door open.

Racks of clothing and displays blocked her from having a clear view of Ben's office, and she stepped to the side. Her arm hit a box, and it clattered to the floor.

Destiny Unknown

Sucking in a breath, she waited, not moving. If it was the security guard, he should say something.

Instead of a voice, she heard footsteps—hurried footsteps—going in the opposite direction.

"Hey!" Bernadette yelled, and started toward Shipping and Receiving. She heard the clank of the outside door and broke into a run. Whoever had been in that office was getting away.

Only moments after the side door closed, she threw it open again and stepped out into the alleyway that separated Morgan's from the next building. A blast of cold air hit her, and she stopped.

A halogen light above her head cast a yellow-green glow over the area and clearly illuminated the gray van parked next to the curb. The name *Grand Cleaning* was painted on its side. Once a month Bernadette signed a check to that company. According to Anne, they'd been cleaning Morgan's for years.

"Hello?" Bernadette called out.

Silence answered her call.

"Anybody out here?" she asked, not quite as loudly. Tension rippled through her, and she checked behind her, not sure if she wanted to be outside or in.

She thought she heard a rattling sound, then a car passed by the end of the alley, a lone traveler on a near-deserted street. Holding her breath, Bernadette listened for any sounds in the alley.

What she heard was the thud of her heart and the hum of the light above her head. Then she heard footsteps.

They came from the sidewalk in front of the store. Slow, ambling steps. The gait of someone in no rush, yet someone who had a destination in mind. Someone who didn't mind the cold, or the darkness, or how deserted the downtown area was at midnight.

She waited, mesmerized by the sound, her gaze fixed in that direction. She wasn't surprised when the figure of a man rounded the side of the store and started down the alleyway. For a moment he was no more than a shadowy silhouette.

Then she recognized him.

"What are you doing here?" she called to Cody.

"Looking for you." He didn't pick up his pace. "What are you doing here?"

Good question, she thought, glancing around the alley. *Acting like an idiot*, came to mind. *Scaring myself.* "I've been working," she said.

"And I thought Parker was a workaholic. You do this on a regular basis?"

"No." And she doubted she'd do it again. Another glance in the direction of the cleaning van assured her no one was there, and Bernadette stepped back into the store, holding the door open for Cody. "You weren't in here—in the store—just a few minutes ago, were you?"

He shook his head. "I've been in that meeting all evening." He pointed toward the street. "Over at the Amway. In fact, I was driving out of the garage when I saw your car. Kind of surprised me, so I thought I'd see what was up. I tried the front doors. They were locked, so I decided I'd try this door."

"When you were trying the front doors, did you see anyone come running out of the alley? Maybe Ben?"

"No." Cody cocked his head, a frown crossing his brow. "Why?"

"Because someone just left the store through this door." She nodded toward the one she held open. "Left running."

Cody looked down at her. "And you came chasing after him?"

"I wanted to see who it was."

"And what if it had been a burglar?" His gaze slid over her coat to the slacks she'd slipped on earlier that evening, to her low heels. "What were you going to do if you caught him? Take him on bare-handed?"

"All right, I wasn't thinking." Cody's attitude irked her, in part because he was right. She wouldn't have had any way to defend herself. "Look, as long as you're here, would you mind sticking around a few minutes?" She stepped back into the store. "I'd like to check Ben's office."

"Now you're turning into a spy?"

"Just being a general manager." She smiled. "If someone was in Ben's office, I need to know if anything was taken."

Cody knew what she wanted—a chance to look around Ben's office to see if she could find any evidence to connect Ben with the problems she'd been having. Not that Cody blamed her. In her position he'd do the same.

He followed her toward the two offices just off Shipping and Receiving. Large glass windows separated the offices from the work area, and the interiors of each room were dark. Bernadette tried the door closest to the sales floor, found it locked, and glanced his way. "I'm sure the light was on in Ben's office, not Loren's."

"Whoever was in there could have locked the door when he left."

"Could have." She pulled a set of keys from her purse and slid one into the lock. Immediately the door opened, and she snapped on a light and entered the room.

A four-drawer file cabinet stood in the far corner of the room, and a huge planning calendar hung on one wall. Two office chairs flanked a massive desk that held In and Out file holders, a printer, a fax machine, a scanner, and a computer. A spaceship with a cartoon figure floated across the monitor of the computer. Bernadette pointed at the screen. "Look, he didn't have a chance to turn off his computer."

"Some people leave theirs on all the time." The screen saver indicated Ben might be one. "Did you get your e-mail off to Parker?"

"I did. I told him all was fine and dandy." She began shuffling through the papers on the desk. "I'd love to know what message Ben sent Parker."

Cody stared at the spaceship as it floated in a new pattern across the screen. "From what Loren told me the other night, there's a way to find out. I gather he's somewhat of a hacker. I have no idea, however, how to come up with someone's password."

"Nor I."

Finished with the papers on the desk, Bernadette tried the drawers. They were locked. Next she went to the file cabinet. One by one, she tested those drawers, none yielding to her efforts. She faced Cody. "I thought maybe, since I interrupted what he was doing, he might not have had a chance to lock up."

"That's assuming it was Ben you interrupted." It bothered Cody to think of the danger she might have been in.

She glanced around the office, her shoulders sagging perceptibly. "I don't know what to do now. Everything's going wrong—"

Cody heard the crack in her voice. She'd stopped

herself, but a slight tremble in her chin relayed her fears. He could almost hear her telling herself she wouldn't lose control. "Hey," he said, stepping closer. "You'll figure this out."

"Right." She smiled, but it was forced.

"You're not alone."

He slipped his arms around her shoulders and drew her close. That she didn't pull back but leaned into him was encouraging. He wanted to help her—knew she needed his help—if only she'd let down the barriers.

He felt her tremble in his arms. Gently he tipped up her chin. "You okay?"

She nodded, her gaze locked on his face. Her eyes were the blue of a summer day, and in them he saw a longing that matched his. When she licked her lips, he knew neither of them was okay. From the first time they'd met, she'd created a yearning in him. Maybe she wasn't the princess in his sister's story, but Bernadette was special. Leaning his head closer, he claimed her lips.

Her mouth moved with his, open and giving, asking and receiving. He explored her lips, then her cheeks and her throat. Her coat and his jacket were open, and he found a way under her sweater to the warmth of her skin, even as she pulled at his shirt, drawing it free from his jeans. Soft, warm flesh slid under his fingers until he came to a silky barrier. First he explored, circling the smooth mounds of her breasts, then he rubbed his palms over the hard nubs that peaked each. Her groan was his signal to go on, to search out the clasp that held her captive.

As he freed her breasts, she slid her hands under his shirt, the delicate touch of her fingers triggering the tightening of his muscles and the constriction of his stomach. He kissed her deep, his tongue parrying with hers. The blood pooled in his loins, the need for a release growing uncomfortably strong. She rubbed her hips against his, moaning and whether or not they would make love ceased to be the question. Where was now the problem. He drew his head back and glanced around the small office.

Through the window looking out on Shipping and Receiving, he saw the door they'd come through earlier begin to open. Immediately he stilled, his arms tightening around Bernadette. "Someone's coming into the store," he whispered near her ear.

Her body stiffened. "Who?" she asked, the word a strangled groan.

"I'm not sure." But he was sure they were at a disadvantage. The light they'd turned on illuminated them clearly while the figure in the doorway was no more than a silhouette.

Quickly, Bernadette disengaged her hands from under his shirt. Pulling her coat closed in front of her, she faced the doorway. Cody heard her sigh. "It's the security guard."

She stepped away from him, touching her hair as she did. Cody watched. Not a strand was out of place, yet she fussed. The guard walked toward Ben's office, and she opened the door before he reached it. "Where have you been?" she demanded, overriding any question the guard might have had.

The man stopped, his gaze jumping between her and Cody. His expression was curious, but he kept his words cautious. "I was checking the outside of the building."

"Someone was in this office," Bernadette said, her tone stern. "No more than five minutes ago. He ran out when I came down from my office. You didn't see anything?"

"Nothing." The man glanced around the office. "I must have been on the other side of the building. Was anything taken?"

"We were just checking." She glanced Cody's way. "This is a friend of mine."

The security guard nodded, then looked back at her. "None of the doors were open when I checked."

"And you're sure you saw no one? Maybe one of the employees? Perhaps Mr. Waite?"

"No one," the guard said firmly.

"Then I suggest you check Shipping and Receiving thoroughly, because someone was down here, someone who didn't want to be seen."

Her facade of control firmly in place, she said to Cody, "We might as well go. This is what we're paying him to do."

Cody followed her lead, nodding toward the security guard as they passed. It wasn't until they were in the alleyway, the door closed behind them, that Bernadette released a sigh and laughed uneasily. "Nothing like being found in a compromising position."

Cody caught her arm, stopping her progress toward the street and their cars. "It wasn't as compromising as it could have been."

She stared at him, her gaze darting from his earrings, to his gold chain, to his jeans. Quickly she looked back up at his face. "I don't know what it is. Every time I'm around you—"

"We both know what it is," he said, through playing games. "I want to make love with you, and I think you want to make love with me."

The light above the door gave her skin a greenish tinge, and Cody wondered if Dumb John had been this aroused by his green princess. Fairy tales didn't deal with hormones, only morals, and what he was thinking was definitely immoral. "Come to my place."

NINE

Bernadette kept her gaze on the truck ahead, its taillights glowing like twin bouncing rubies on a backdrop of empty streets and murky darkness. She could still change her mind, she told herself. If she wanted, she could turn around and head for her apartment. There was no cable linking Cody's truck to her car, no reason she had to make every turn he made. She was in control of her life.

In complete control.

"Right," she said aloud, then laughed at the irony.

Control was when you planned your actions and reactions and behaved accordingly. Control meant the unexpected didn't come strolling down an alley and almost lure you into making love in a coworker's office.

The muscles in her stomach tightened, and she smiled into the darkness. It had been a long time since a man had excited her as much as Cody did. Too damn long.

Tonight she would spend a few hours in his company, relieve some of the tension. This was sex and nothing more. Sleeping with Cody had nothing to do with love or relationships or silly fairy tales. Nothing at all.

Cody got out of his truck and waited as Bernadette turned off her car's lights and grabbed her purse. His insides were coiled as tight as a spring, but he kept his posture relaxed. That she'd come amazed him. When she'd insisted on taking her own car and following him, he'd been sure she would change her mind and make a beeline for her apartment as soon as they left the parking garage.

All the way from the store to his place, he'd kept glancing into his rearview mirror, waiting for those headlights to veer off. The closer they came to his drive, the greater his anxiety. Now he didn't know what to say.

She stepped up beside him. He sucked in a deep breath of cold night air and looked up at the cloud-covered sky. "Think spring will ever come?"

"No."

The one word was all she gave, and he glanced down at her face. His yard light had come on automatically as they'd neared the house. It illuminated her features, but didn't penetrate beneath those long lashes and cool blue eyes. How he would love to know what she was thinking. Feeling. Were her insides as quivery as his?

He slid an arm around her shoulders, drawing her close. "Come on, let's get inside where it's warmer."

Together they walked up the stone steps to his carved doors. Once inside, he took her coat and hung it on a hook, then removed his own jacket. Nervously he rubbed his hands together and glanced toward the kitchen. "Would you like something to drink? Wine? Coffee?"

"No."

Again it was just the one word. She wasn't going to make this easy for him. Usually a woman asked for something, even if she didn't want it and never drank it. The act of fixing a drink allowed a little time, switched the focus of why they were there, and gave them something to talk about. Now he was left with silence. He looked toward the back door. "I'm surprised Thor didn't bark when we pulled up."

"Where is your dog?" she asked.

"Outside." Cody walked to one of the back windows. "He has a kennel. When I have to be away a long time and can't take him with me, I put him out there."

Thor was in the kennel, staring toward the house. Cody knew the dog expected him to step outside any minute. He wouldn't understand being left out all night.

There were a lot of things Cody didn't understand.

Slowly he walked back to Bernadette. "He's got a thick coat. He'll be fine."

"Mopsy's probably wondering where I am. I never knew how possessive and demanding a dog could be. And I never thought I'd be sleeping with a dog."

"I've been called worse."

She smiled for the first time. "You know what I mean."

He knew. He also remembered she'd once said she didn't like dogs. "You actually sleep with her?"

Bernadette shrugged. "It wasn't something I planned. In fact, six months ago if you'd told me I'd be sleeping with a dog, I would have told you, you were crazy."

"People change. Preconceived ideas can change." His had certainly changed about her.

She lifted her eyebrows, and he knew she understood. "What about you? Do you sleep with your dog?"

"No. And don't ask why."

Again the eyebrows went up. "Now you've made me curious."

"Sleep with me and I'll tell you."

He held out his hand, but she didn't take it. Her gaze traveled up the steps, then back to his face. "I don't know. Maybe this isn't a good idea."

He saw the apprehension in her eyes. He felt a little that way himself. "Something gets lost, doesn't it, when you have to drive ten miles to find a bed? Some of the spontaneity . . . the loss of control."

Immediately her chin went up. "You think I always have to be in control, don't you?"

"Don't you?"

She shook her head. "It's not a matter of control, it's just that I don't like making mistakes."

"Do you think this is a mistake?" He touched her cheek, grazing the backs of his fingers over velvety smooth skin.

"Probably." She put a hand over his. "All we're talking about is tonight, right? Just tonight. I don't want you to think—"

"That this is some fairy tale?" He nodded. "I understand."

Bernadette wished she did. She wanted to run, to escape before it was too late, but she stood where she was, trapped by the sweet desire she saw in his eyes and a matching need within herself. "We're both mature adults."

"Very mature."

She glared at him. "You're making fun of me."

Destiny Unknown

"No, but I don't think we need to rationalize what we're about to do."

Bern did, though. She needed a rational reason. "I'm not exactly a hot lover."

He chuckled. "I don't believe that. You certainly weren't the ice princess in Ben's office."

"That, ah—" was something she couldn't explain.

"That was just the beginning," he said, and swooped her off her feet.

"What are you doing?" she cried, automatically wrapping her arms around his neck.

"Carrying you up the stairs."

He made it sound so normal. "You can't."

"I think I am."

"You'll hurt yourself, pull something."

He laughed. "I must admit, you're not as light as I thought you'd be."

She stiffened. "Put me down!"

"A little touchy about your weight?"

"My weight is perfectly fine."

"Everything about you is perfectly fine."

"Sure, that's what you think now. Cody, you're going to injure yourself. This is crazy. You're crazy."

"That's what my stepbrothers always say. You know what? Maybe I am."

They reached the top of the stairs, but Cody didn't put her down. She pulled in her legs when he carried her through the doorway of his bedroom, and she laughed when she saw his bed. "Oh great, Romeo. Are we going to make love or spend the night reading?"

"We," he said breathlessly, "are going to make love."

He set her down next to his bed and quickly grabbed the books scattered across his comforter. Bernadette noticed some of the titles. *Laws and Rules Relating to Resi-*

dential Builders. Michigan Administrative Code. Michigan Compiled Laws. "A little light reading?"

"Part of the job."

The stack he piled on his lamp stand fell over, and he grinned her way. "That's how I got my name. Dumb John. The clumsy one."

"You're not clumsy," she said, and helped him with the books.

"I am around you." He threw himself on top of the comforter face up, as if testing the mattress. "Clumsy. Awkward. And completely dumbfounded."

"Dumbfounded?" she repeated, feeling awkward herself and not quite sure what to do other than stand by the bed looking down at him.

"Dumbfounded. Baffled." He reached up and pulled her down on top of him.

"Cody!"

"That's my name."

He shifted his weight on the bed, positioning her so her hips were on his, his arousal unmistakable. His expression turned serious. "I didn't think you'd come tonight."

She knew the joking had ended. The hesitancy in his voice said he was as unsure as she felt. "I couldn't seem to stop myself."

No more than she could stop herself from leaning forward and touching her lips to his, from letting her fingers explore his hair and trace the outline of his left ear, finding each of the gold loops that pierced the lobe. "What is it about you? From that first day in the veterinarian's office, you've had me confused and . . . and—"

"Horny?"

She could feel the bulge under his zipper. Leaning

Destiny Unknown

back, she grinned. "I think that's a word that better fits you."

"No doubt about it." With the agility of a cat, he turned her so she was under him and he was the one on top.

She laughed. "I should have known you wouldn't let me stay in control."

"You've been in control for the last two weeks, have been driving me out of my mind, and now I'm going to make love to you, Bernadette Sanders." He spread her legs with his knees. "*To* you and *with* you. I want to know you from the inside out, to be a part of you."

To know you is to love you, her grandmother had always said. But when people knew her, they left. Her mother. Her father. Even Parker.

She said nothing.

Cody's hands moved to her hair, and the pins that held her efficient, businesslike twist in place fell away. He combed his fingers through the freed tresses, fanning them out around her face, then lifting one strand of pale gold and another, letting each sift through his fingers. "Your hair is like silk," he said, and smiled. "Your skin like velvet."

His gaze dropped to her sweater, and through the soft cashmere fibers he touched her breasts, first one, then the other. Her nipples hardened and, like eager children wanting to be recognized, pressed against her bra and his palm. In her car she'd resnapped her bra. Now it was too confining.

Cody pulled her sweater up and over her head. Casually he tossed it aside, then concentrated on her bra, the nylon cups revealing more than they concealed. She tried not to respond when he slowly dragged one finger over the soft swell of her breast, but it was impossible to ignore the muscles tightening between her legs and the quivering sensation in her stomach. He reached around and once again released the clasp of her bra, then, for a moment, simply stared at her breasts.

She touched his face, cradling it in her hands, then guided his mouth to the objects of his regard. Like a man starved for nourishment, he fastened on a nipple, sucking greedily. She, too, was starved. Gasping at her own reaction, she slid her hands through his hair, holding him to her.

Only when he'd drawn from both of her nipples did he pause. Sitting back on his haunches, he stared at her, his hair disheveled from the exploration of her hands. He looked like a wild man, but his hesitant touch was gentle and civilized. "Why is it I like everything about you?" he asked, his husky voice hinting at the fragility of his control.

"Do you?" She wasn't so naive as to believe a man in the throes of passion.

"Oh, yes. I like the way you look, and the way you move. I even like the way you talk, especially when you smile and laugh. It's cute the way you try not to show any emotions, pretend you don't care."

She didn't want to be thought of as cute, and she didn't like the emotions he was touching. "Maybe I'm not pretending."

"If that's what you think, then your actions are calling you a liar."

"Maybe you're seeing what you want to see, but when you really get to know me—"

"What?"

"What?" was the question she couldn't answer. What made men leave her? What did she lack?

Bernadette shook her head. Cody couldn't leave because she wasn't going to stay. This was for tonight, and only for tonight. A tryst. Wasn't that what her grandmother called it? A one-night stand was probably a better description. "Are you going to make love to me or talk?"

"I am going to make love to you," he said with total conviction.

There was clothing to be dealt with, however. Hers. His. Her sweater and bra were already lying by the side of the bed. She pulled at his shirt, tossing it aside. He asked for the lights out. She objected. "I want to see you."

He chuckled and commanded the lights back on.

Next came her shoes and slacks. Getting undressed wasn't a quick endeavor. The removal of each item was paired with a kiss. His boots were good for two. Two long kisses that made her blood simmer. After that came his jeans. They were down to her pantyhose and panties, and his socks and briefs. Of course, the gold chain remained around his neck. She knew without saying that the chain would stay.

Arching over her, he teasingly rubbed his hips against hers. She groaned, pressing her palms against his chest. If the gesture was meant to stop him, she forgot the objective as soon as she touched the mat of brown hairs that tapered to his briefs. If she was silk and velvet, he was the earth, solid and strong.

Again he rubbed himself over her, and she slid her hands around his neck, positive he was driving her insane. When his fingertips slipped under the waistband of her pantyhose, she automatically lifted her hips, allowing him the freedom to completely strip her. Next went his briefs. He eased on a shield of protection, and she silently thanked him and admonished herself for not thinking of that. The wild need pulsating through her had wiped out all coherent thoughts. Somewhere along the way, she had lost control, and it no longer seemed to matter.

He pressed himself against her, probing greedily for the moist warmth of her desire. Closing her eyes, she wrapped her arms and legs around him, taking him in, his need a hard shaft of primitive impulses. She cried out against her will, the sound a surprised gasp, and he stilled, holding himself where he was.

"No." She groaned, not wanting him to stop. "It's all right. It's just been a long time."

"I'm glad." He kissed her neck and her shoulder, and nuzzled her cheek. "So very glad." He kept kissing her, nibbling and licking various spots on her face and neck . . . giving her time for her body to accept him.

She reached down to touch him, but he caught her hand. "No. It's been a long time for me too. How much control I have, I'm not really sure."

Yet when he again moved, his thrusts were controlled, each going just a little deeper, slowly stretching her to accept him. For a moment she saw the analogy—that her body was resisting even as her mind had, but in the end giving in. She started to smile, then didn't have time. A searing kiss stole away her breath, his lips igniting a fire only one thing could quench. She knew the time for gentleness and control was over.

Why making love with Cody was different, she wasn't sure. The anatomy was the same, the basics of kissing and touching, the thrusts and retreats. It wasn't as though she'd done it a thousand times before, but she had made love enough to consider herself experienced, perhaps even jaded. She'd been prepared to put on the show, to make the right sounds. She hadn't been prepared for the sizzling heat that surged through her, or the molten sensations that turned her wet and hot.

She'd never known this desperate urgency that took her breath away and erased all possibility of control, not even her first time, in the backseat of Parker's car, when both of them had been crazy with desire and scared to death they might be caught. She'd never known making love could be so frenzied and wild. Cody had unleashed something untameable, and it both frightened and excited her.

The throbbing of his climax took her beyond pleasure. She heard his voice, felt the room spin, and dug her fingernails into his back. Squeezing her legs tight against his thighs, her cry rising as a sob of submission, she shook under him, the waves of release leaving her totally vulnerable.

Only slowly did the tension ebb, a sweet exhaustion taking its place, her body melting into the comforter. "Yes," he murmured into her ear, giving her one more kiss, this one tender and brief.

He eased himself to her side and pulled the comforter up so its edge covered her. Cuddling her close, he nuzzled her hair and blew soft kisses against her forehead, murmuring something she didn't catch.

She didn't ask him to repeat it, afraid to trust her voice. The emotions welling inside of her threatened to spill over and expose her. He'd touched her in a way she hadn't expected, had discovered a part of her she'd never known existed. Lovemaking had never been that raw, that free, not for her. The need had never been that desperate.

In silence she stared up at the ceiling. What could she say to him? What was he thinking?

Had he felt what she'd felt?

She waited, expecting him to speak. She heard the rhythm of his breathing slow and deepen, and she knew there would be no conversation, no purging of the mind and baring of the soul. William Cody Taylor was asleep.

Obviously what they'd just experienced hadn't affected him the same way it had affected her. What a fool she was. What an idiotic fool.

Careful not to wake him, Bernadette slipped out from under the comforter and off his bed. She grabbed her scattered clothes and tiptoed into the bathroom, pulling the door closed behind her. For a moment she stood in the dark, then she ventured a command. "Light on," she said, and the light came on.

The whirlpool at the far end of the room looked tempting, especially since her body still felt sensitive and tense, but she knew she didn't dare the luxury of bathing. Quickly she dressed. If all went well, she would be gone by the time Cody awoke. Then there would be no need for explanations, no need for talk. Oh, he'd be upset. He would probably show up tomorrow morning at her office or her apartment demanding an explanation, but by then she'd have some answers. By then she would understand what had happened.

Those were her plans, but when she reached the bottom of his stairs, she knew her legs weren't going to take her any farther, not as weak as they felt. Sinking down on the bottom step, she hugged her knees to her chest and buried her face against them. Raw emotions poured out, the floodgate opened. Control was the mainstay of her life, and somehow she'd lost it.

She wasn't aware of Cody, not until he sat beside her and slipped an arm around her shoulders, drawing her close. His body still held the scent of their lovemaking, and she squeezed her lids tighter, willing him to disappear. Nothing was going right tonight. Nothing had gone right for the last two weeks.

"I'm sorry," he said, and she heard the remorse in his voice. "Just call me Dumb John."

She said nothing, afraid to speak.

"Only an oaf falls asleep after something that wonderful."

"Don't—" The one thing she didn't want was a lie.

"You were leaving. Why?"

"I need to get home." Away from the danger he posed. "Mopsy—"

"Did you leave papers on the floor?"

She could lie about that, but she didn't. "Yes."

"Then Mopsy's fine."

But Bernadette wasn't. Cody knew from the tears and the tautness in her voice and body that she was anything but fine. "Did I hurt you?"

"No." She glanced his way, then back at a spot somewhere between the toes of her tan pumps.

"Did I say something I shouldn't have?" It wouldn't be the first time.

"No." She kept her gaze on that spot.

"Then why were you leaving?"

"I have to." The desperation was still there. "We agreed. This was just for tonight."

"The night's young." And sitting beside her, he knew his need for her hadn't lessened.

"It's late." Once again she looked at him. "Please, Cody, don't make this any more difficult than it has to be."

"And why does it have to be difficult at all?" Her responses to him in his bedroom certainly hadn't come from indifference. Unless she was a consummate actress, what they'd just shared had been as spectacular for her as it had been for him. "Stay the night. Let me get to know you better."

"Why? We did it. It was good. Let's leave it at that."

"Maybe it can be better. Maybe it doesn't have to be for just one night."

Her eyebrows rose. "What are you suggesting? An affair? A long-term relationship?"

He wasn't sure what he was suggesting, he simply didn't want her to go home.

"And what do I do when you decide to leave?" she asked. "Pretend again that it doesn't hurt?"

She bit her lower lip, quickly looking away, and he suspected she hadn't meant to let that slip out. "What makes you think I'll leave?"

"Because it happens."

A simple answer. He'd bet there was more. "When has it happened?"

He received a glance, nothing more. Her reluctance to talk was clear, but he'd run up against that reluctance before. Persistence, he knew, was his best weapon. "Who left you?"

"Others."

That was a start. "I want names."

"Why?"

"Because this is something we need to get out in the open."

"We don't need to get anything out in the open. My coming here tonight was a mistake. Now I'm leaving."

She started to rise to her feet. He caught her hand, stopping her. "Bern. You can't keep running. And you can't pretend there's nothing between us."

"And why not?" She remained poised between standing and sitting, his hold balancing her as she pulled against him. "I keep pretending my father loves me. Pre-

Destiny Unknown

tending I'm in control of my life. You want to know why you'll leave?" Her gaze was locked on his face, her eyes a watery blue. "I don't know why. It just happens. If I let myself love someone, they either die or leave. Even if I don't love someone, they leave. Maybe it's my fault, I don't know." Her chin trembled. "After a while you learn to protect yourself. Maybe I drive them off . . . or maybe I'm cursed."

She did have demons, he mused, and he wished they were living a fairy tale. How much easier it would be if he could simply keep his mouth shut and end the spell, banish the demons. His silence, however, wouldn't chase away her self-doubts. "You're too intelligent to believe in curses."

"You believe in fairy tales."

"I believe in what fairy tales teach you."

She rolled her eyes. "And what did you learn? That women who wear green need your help?"

If so, Bernadette was resisting his help. "The point my sister was trying to make when she told me that story was, don't listen to what others say because it might not be true. Believe in what you know." Cody rose, keeping a tenuous balance between them, his grip on her arm never loosening. "It took me a while to accept that idea, especially with so many around me making fun of me, but you know what? It's true. My stepbrothers and stepfather are all architects. They don't take chances, don't bungle jobs, and don't fail. They've never had wild and fanciful daydreams, and I doubt anyone has ever called an idea they had dumb. But I'm now worth twice what the three of them are worth together, and I believe in myself."

"Give the man another gold star."

Cody shook his head, afraid there was no way to get

through to her. "I think you're right. I think you do drive people away."

"So let me go." She looked down at his hand on her arm.

"Your wish is my command, Princess." He released his hold slowly so that she wouldn't lose her balance, then he bowed.

TEN

Bernadette overslept. She never overslept, but then, she never stayed up half the night making love when she knew she had to be at work the next morning. She never did any of the things she'd done lately, and going to work with her hair down was as symptomatic of her mental state as her lack of time that morning. She knew it was a mistake the moment she saw Ben.

He was talking to Kevin Lutz, the head of the men's department. As Bernadette walked down the aisle toward the escalator, she felt their gazes. The way they were looking at her, she wouldn't have been surprised to discover her skin had turned green. Chin high, she veered toward them. Control came only from facing situations, and she needed to regain control.

"Were you in your office last night?" she asked as she neared the two men, her question clearly directed at Ben. "Late last night. Around midnight."

The smile Ben gave her was close to a smirk, and she knew he'd heard she'd been in his office, and not alone. She'd expected he'd know. How much that security guard had seen and related was the question. Too much, she was sure.

"I left the store right after I called you last night," Ben said. He gave Kevin a quick glance, and Bernadette knew Ben's absence from his office and her presence in it—with a man—was exactly what the two had been discussing.

"Someone was in your office," she said.

Ben's attention came back to her, his smile most definitely a smirk. "So I understand."

She went on as if she hadn't noticed. "I came back here last night and sent an e-mail to Parker and Effie, then caught up on some work. It was close to midnight when I left my office. I talked to two of the women on the cleaning staff." They would verify she'd been alone then, and she hoped Ben questioned them. "It was when I was coming down the escalator that I noticed the light on in your office."

"Could have been more of the cleaning staff," Ben said.

"My thoughts exactly . . . until the light went off and whoever was in there took off through the side door at a run."

Ben looked toward Shipping and Receiving and the side door. A frown replaced the smirk. "What about security?"

"Evidently it's not as good as we've thought. The guard didn't show up until a friend of mine and I had checked out your office."

"Friend?" As quickly as it had disappeared, Ben's smile returned, and he glanced at Kevin.

"Friend," she repeated firmly. "He'd been at a meeting at the Amway Hotel and just happened by when I was chasing down this intruder. Thank goodness he was around. I wanted to check out your office, but I wasn't wild about doing it alone. Not that we could tell if anything was missing. What about you? When you got in this morning, did you notice anything missing?"

"No." Ben studied her face, and Bernadette knew he was weighing her version of the incident against whatever the security guard had reported.

"Did you notice anything out of the ordinary?"

He shook his head. "No."

"Well, I think we'd better get Security to keep a closer watch on your office." She nodded at Kevin, then started for the escalator, satisfied that she was leaving in control of the situation.

That feeling lasted three steps. "Nice hairdo," Ben called after her. "Sexy."

Pausing, she looked back at the two men. Both were grinning. She gave them an icy glare. "Thank you."

By the time she reached her office, Bernadette wondered if she would have attracted as much attention if she'd come to work without any clothes on. Over half of the sales staff had made some sort of comment about her hair. "I simply overslept and didn't have time to put my hair up," she told Anne before she had a chance to say anything.

Anne nodded and handed Bernadette her mail. "I understand you thought someone was in Ben's office last night."

"News travels fast." But she'd learned that after nine years in the business. "I didn't *think* I saw someone, I did see someone."

"And?" Anne waited for her to identify the person.

Bernadette wished she could. "That's basically it. Whoever it was got away before I could see him."

"Do you have any idea what he was doing? Is anything missing? Was anything broken into?"

"No." That was the confusion. "Ben's files were still locked, and he says nothing's missing. The only thing out of the ordinary was, his computer was on." And she hadn't asked him if he'd left it on.

"Maybe he leaves it on all the time."

It was the same thing Cody had said. Bernadette didn't want to think about Cody. "Maybe."

She hoped Ben would say he'd turned his computer off before leaving the store. A call to his office dashed that possibility. He always left his computer on during the week, he told her. Didn't turn it off except when he'd be gone for a day or two, which would be tomorrow and Friday, since he was working the weekend.

"But no one can get into my files," he added. "Not without my password."

"Loren said passwords aren't infallible."

"Nothing is missing," Ben said.

Something was missing, she thought. Either Ben had come back and she'd nearly caught him, or someone else had been in his office. And if it was Ben, what could he have been doing that he couldn't have admitted? All he would have had to say was that he was working late. He wouldn't have needed to run off. Not unless he was trying to hide something.

Bernadette mulled over the questions for almost an hour. After that, she didn't have time to think about it. Since a fashion show without models was difficult to pull off, the call she received from the assistant manager at the Twenty-eighth Street store turned that problem into a priority.

Morgan's Spring Fashion Show was part of their annual "After-School Special" promotion. It was sched-

Destiny Unknown

uled to begin at four o'clock that afternoon, and Mary Elizabeth Delgato, the assistant manager at the Twenty-eighth Street store, didn't find out until ten o'clock that morning that no models had been hired.

Actually, the models should have been hired, and once Bernadette received the call from Mary, she contacted the modeling agency that always supplied their models to find out what had gone wrong. The answer she received wasn't one she wanted to hear. As before, the guilt appeared to rest on her shoulders. The modeling agency swore she was the one who'd canceled the contract. They had the letter of cancellation—with her signature—in the file.

Setting the telephone in its cradle, she leaned back in her chair and closed her eyes. "You're in control," she repeated to herself, then laughed. She wasn't in control. Not of her life, her job, or her emotions.

She'd run out of Cody's house the night before like a scared rabbit. Making love with him had been the biggest mistake of her life. The tension hadn't been eased. Nothing was better.

He'd touched emotions in her too raw to expose. For years, she'd protected herself, had avoided situations that might make her vulnerable. How she'd walked into this one, she would never know. One minute she knew where she was going, the next she was making out in a coworker's office and going home with a man she barely knew, a man who turned her inside out. Twice in the last two weeks she'd cried in his arms. She never cried. Twice she'd told him things she hadn't confessed even to her sister. People saw her as strong and capable, sure of herself.

Cody now knew it was all a facade.

Of all people, why had she let down her hair with him?

Bernadette touched her hair, running her fingers through it. Less than twelve hours ago Cody had been running his fingers through her hair, tangling it in his grasp. He'd been kissing her, sucking on her breasts . . . making love with her. Just the thought of it had her quivering inside, wanting. He'd turned her into a wanton woman, starved for sex.

Wiggling uncomfortably in her chair, she knew she couldn't sit in her office thinking about Cody Taylor. She'd left him last night so that he wouldn't leave her. Now she had to get him out of her thoughts. She needed to be doing something.

"I'll be at the Twenty-eighth Street store," she told Anne, and headed out of the downtown store.

"They'll do." Mary Elizabeth Delgato nodded her approval to Bernadette. "That was quick thinking on your part."

"Something had to be done." Bernadette watched the coed from Grand Rapids Junior College make a turn in front of the customers watching her. Bern's call to the Drama Department had provided the models they needed, even if the girls' figures weren't standard and a few were women instead of teenagers. You didn't complain when you had only a few hours to come up with a miracle.

One miracle, however, didn't erase the doubts she was sure Mary had. Bernadette wanted the woman to understand what had happened. "I didn't cancel the other models, no matter what the agency says. Something's going on, something I haven't been able to put my finger on, but I'll figure it out soon enough."

Mary nodded and smiled. "I understand you found someone in Ben's office last night."

The gossip had traveled to this store as well. In a way, that was good. Better to squelch the rumors now. "I saw a light on in Ben's office, and someone went running out of the area when I got near. I didn't actually 'find' anyone."

"I heard he has long hair and wears earrings." Mary looked toward the front of the misses' department. "That wouldn't happen to be him, would it?"

Bernadette followed Mary's gaze. She hoped Mary was wrong, but she wasn't really surprised to see Cody lounging against a sweater display. He looked the same as usual, in his leather jacket and threadbare jeans, his long hair and three gold earrings. The gold chain wasn't visible, but she knew it was around his neck, symbolically reminding him to believe in himself.

The only thing different, she noticed, were his eyes. They were bloodshot. So were hers. Lack of sleep did that to her.

The warmth that dashed through her at the sight of him wasn't welcome. She wanted to ignore him, but knew he wouldn't remain quietly in the background. It wasn't his way. Her only choice was to go to him. She nodded to Mary and started for Cody.

"What brings you here?" she asked before she reached the display of sweaters Cody was resting against.

"You." His gaze followed the flow of her hair. "You left it down."

She didn't like the intimacy of his gaze or the mention of her hairstyle. "You left it down" could be interpreted a lot of ways, and with the rumors circulating as they were, she was sure she wouldn't like any interpretation. She lowered her voice. "I thought we settled matters last night."

"I'd say matters are very unsettled." He glanced in Mary's direction. "Would you like to discuss this over a cup of coffee?"

At least he was acknowledging that this wasn't the proper place to be having a discussion of this nature, and getting him out of the store and away from the staff's watchful eyes would be better than arguing with him on the sales floor. The fashion show seemed to be proceeding without a hitch now that they had models to wear the outfits. Mary could handle matters on her own. Bernadette gave in to Cody. "If that's what you want."

"You know what I want."

The huskiness of his voice said volumes, and Bernadette hurried toward the closest exit. She did know what he wanted. What was driving her crazy was the fact that she also wanted it. One night hadn't been enough. Considering how she'd come apart in his arms, she wondered if she could ever get enough.

Like anything sinful, he was addictive. And he wouldn't go away. "Why did you come here?" she demanded the moment they were out of the store.

"Anne said you were here working on a problem. Something about no models."

"Another of those cancellations with my signature that I'm sure I never initiated."

"And that's why I'm here."

She cocked her head, not following him.

"I was thinking about those signatures of yours that keep popping up," he said. "Could you get one of the originals?"

"I suppose." If the Grand Rapids *Press* wouldn't give

Destiny Unknown

her the original verification on last week's ad, she was sure the modeling agency would supply that so-called letter of cancellation. There was also the signature card at the bank. Then again, considering the suspicious way Frank had acted yesterday, he might not be willing to hand over his one piece of evidence that would positively link her to that account. "The modeling agency has one. I probably could get it," she said. "Why?"

"On Saturday, Katrina, the electrician I like to work with, is going to be at my place. She's into handwriting analysis and should be able to tell you if the signature is yours or a forgery. If you could come by—"

"You want me to go to your place?"

Her voice and expression revealed her distress, but Cody hadn't expected otherwise. She wanted to forget he existed, and if he had any sense, he would stay out of her life. But the memory of last night was too fresh in his mind. He'd made love before, but never like that. Bernadette was different. From the first day they'd met, she'd had him dancing on a string. Now she had that string wrapped around his heart.

He would never forget finding her at the bottom of his stairs, crying. Falling asleep after something as wonderful as they'd shared was unforgivable. Guilt alone would have brought him to her today, but seeing her vulnerability, and hearing her fears had sealed his fate. The ice princess had a reason to protect her emotions. People who got hurt enough times learned to guard themselves. He understood her fears, and he understood why she wouldn't believe things would be different with him. She had no reason to believe him, and it was far better to push someone away than to risk being hurt again.

His sister had pushed everyone away.

He couldn't help Karen, but he could help Bernadette. He needed to, for his sake as well as hers. She could push, but he wouldn't leave, not until he knew for sure that she didn't want him.

And the message he'd gotten in his bed last night hadn't been one of rejection. She'd taken him in with a passion that could have rocked a house off its foundation. He'd filled her, and she'd surrendered all control. Maybe she thought walking away had ended everything, but as far as he was concerned, they were just beginning. Beginning a wonderful journey, destination—destiny—unknown.

Bringing her along required care on his part. Good planning. He kept his tone level. "Let me explain about Saturday. Last year I bought eighty acres and an old farmhouse. The Grand River runs through a portion of the property. What I want to do is develop a residential area on that land that combines private homes with condominiums, a park, and a community center. I have some ideas about how it should look, but I've found that the best guarantee of success is to bring together all the people on the team right at the start, when a project is first being developed. I'm talking about construction bosses, the plumbers and electricians, the lawyers and accountants. Even my PR people. The ideas and insights they have always seem to amaze me. Often they think of things I missed. They're all going to be at my place at one on Saturday. It's a perfect time for you to talk to Katrina and have her look at those signatures. You could even present the problems you've been having to the group. They might catch something you and I have missed."

Bernadette shook her head. "Why can't I just see this

Katrina at her office, and you tell the group about my problems?"

"Katrina won't be in her office for at least a month. She's working on a project up around Marquette. She and one of her assistants are coming down Saturday just for this meeting. They'll spend the night at my place, then head right back up to Marquette on Sunday."

"And I suppose there's no one else around Grand Rapids who can do handwriting analysis?"

He shrugged. "Probably, but no one else that I know. What are you afraid of, Bern? That I'll attack you if you come to my house?"

"No, but—"

"There will be at least a dozen people there. Could be as many as two dozen."

They'd reached the nearby coffee shop, and she waited until they'd each gotten a cup of coffee from the counter and had found a table in the corner before she responded. Voice low, she leaned toward him. "Cody, I told you last night, it would really be better if we didn't see each other again."

"You told me a lot of things last night." He grinned. "You told me you liked it when I nuzzled your neck. That you liked me touching you between your legs. That—"

She didn't let him go on. "You know what I mean."

"Yes, I know what you mean." He reached across the table and covered her hand with his. "I also know that I can't give you reasons why your father takes off for Egypt or why Parker left you, and I don't know why your mother died, but it's not because of you."

She pulled her gaze and her hand away at the same time. "How can you say that? You don't know anything about me."

He laughed. "You're saying that after last night?"

Again she looked at him, the ice back in her eyes. "You don't have to know someone to have sex. Ask a prostitute."

"Is that what it was, Bern? Did you prostitute yourself last night?"

"No, but . . . I— We—" She stared down at her coffee and didn't go on.

He was glad. At least she couldn't lie about what they'd shared. "Look, maybe you're sorry about last night, but I'm not. And you're right, we don't know each other, not well. We've taken the first steps, crossed a few barriers. I'm asking you not to put up any walls."

She kept staring at her cup. "Walls give you boundaries."

"And I don't believe in boundaries. I've made my reputation as a developer by breaking boundaries. I'm the daydreamer I was as a child. I believe in fairy tales and happy endings and finding new ways of looking at situations. I believe in taking chances, even if you might stumble and sometimes fall."

Her head had come up as he talked, her gaze finally meeting his. Silence stretched between them when he finished. He waited, every second increasing his anxiety. She licked her lips and drew in a breath. He said nothing.

Outside the coffee shop, cars were pulling in and out of the parking area, and customers were dashing in for a cup of java to go. Traffic on Twenty-eighth Street was heavy, as usual. Life went on for everyone but Cody. His was held in abeyance by the woman seated across from him.

Finally she spoke. "You're saying that if I go to your place Saturday, nothing will happen?"

Destiny Unknown

He kept his answer to the point. "I'm saying that if you come, you'll meet Katrina and hear what she has to say about that signature. If you want, you can tell the group what's going on and see if they have any ideas. You can stay as long a time or as short a time as you'd like. With luck, you'll leave with some answers. If not, I'll have food and drink there, so you won't go away hungry."

"And you'll be . . . ?"

"Working with the people who will be my employees and teammates for the next two or three years. Brainstorming and planning."

"And that's all?" She cocked her head suspiciously.

"What do you mean, 'Is that all?' I find these sessions extremely important."

"I mean, is that all you and I will be doing? Brainstorming?"

"What do you think?"

ELEVEN

At one-thirty on Saturday afternoon Bernadette steered her white Acura through the grove of trees that hid Cody's "shack" from the main road. Driving from her home to his, she'd thought of a dozen reasons why she shouldn't be doing this. Seeing cars and trucks parked in front of his house, several with business logos on the side, she relaxed a little. It appeared Cody had been honest about this being a business meeting. She'd wondered. He wouldn't be the first man to tell her one thing to get her to his place, only to come up with a quick excuse why they were suddenly alone.

In the coffee shop Wednesday, she'd spent nearly an hour with Cody and had emphasized one point. If she came, it would be strictly because she needed help solving the problems at Morgan's. He was to forget any ideas he might have of her staying and then making love.

Over and over, she'd given him good reasons why they should not see each other again. He'd nodded and smiled and had assured her that she was in control of the situation, that he was only offering a way for her to gain information regarding those mysterious signatures that were popping up all over the place. The control part she doubted, but she had ultimately agreed to come. All morning she'd questioned that decision.

It would have been easy to call and say she wasn't feeling well. It wouldn't even have been a lie. The closer the hour hand on her watch had slipped toward one o'clock, the more queasy her insides had turned. Even now her heart was racing too fast, and butterflies were playing tag in her stomach. She wasn't sure her legs would hold her up to take her to the door.

You're doing this for the store, she told herself. *For Parker, for your job, and for your sanity.* Taking a deep breath, she grabbed her purse and the manila envelope on the seat beside her and stepped out of the car.

The sky was a patchwork of blue and gray, the air the warmest it had been in weeks, and Bernadette saw a robin fly off a bare branch of an apple tree in Cody's front yard. Spring was coming, and she'd dressed accordingly, her pantsuit a lightweight beige wool and her blouse a teal silk. With this outfit, she normally wore a series of gold necklaces and gold hoop earrings. She'd even put them on, but one glance in the mirror had told her to take them off. She would never look at a gold chain again without thinking of the fairy tale Cody's sister had told him. She would never look at gold hoop earrings without thinking of Cody. She'd chosen simple gold studs for her ears and a rope of polished semiprecious stones.

As she started up the stone steps, she wished she'd also chosen heels less than three inches in height. Shaky legs and uneven stones threatened disaster. Holding her purse and the envelope in one hand, she kept her other hand free for balance and took each step slowly.

She'd just reached the carved doors when the roar of a motorcycle engine caught her attention. Turning, she watched the massive machine speed up the drive, its shiny chrome pipes catching the glint of the sun. The motorcycle's black body carried a driver and a passenger, both also clad in black, from boots and jeans to leather jackets and helmets that covered their entire faces. Big and burly, the passenger dwarfed the driver, who parked the deafening machine by the door. The moment they pulled off their helmets, Bernadette understood the size difference. The driver was a woman, the passenger a man. "I see you're late too," the woman called up to her. "Wait for us."

Bernadette waited. Fascinated, she watched the woman run long, slender fingers through short, straight black hair. A quick look in the motorcycle's side mirror prompted her to pull out a tube of lipstick, and in a moment she'd applied a gloss of red.

Her companion was working on his own hair, redoing a ponytail that hung past his shoulders. Once the two were satisfied with their appearance, they headed for the door, taking the stone steps two at a time. "I get to ring the bell," the man said, reaching in front of Bernadette.

"Men. What do you do with them?" the woman said, laughter dancing in her dark eyes. "They're all kids at heart."

From a square speaker box just above the doorbell, a sexy—albeit computerized sounding—female voice asked, "Yes? Who shall I say is calling?"

"Your lover, baby," the man said.

"Just tell Cody we're here," the woman said, and turned to Bernadette.

"Yes? Who shall I say is calling?" the sexy computerized female voice repeated.

"Hi. I'm Kat." The woman in black held out her hand to Bern. "And this sex pervert is Tom. You're?"

"Bernadette."

Kat's handshake was firm, her laugh quick. "Okay, that explains the fancy clothes. You're the store owner. The one Cody said might be here. Did you bring the signatures?"

"You're Katrina?"

The woman didn't look like an electrician or a handwriting analyst. Not that Bernadette knew what a handwriting analyst looked like. She did know that the electricians she'd met had never been pretty and petite.

Any answer she might have given about the signatures died in her throat when the carved doors swung open and Cody stepped into view. He looked like a bum.

He looked wonderful.

Boyish and manly. Cute and sexy. Before her was a living, breathing contradiction.

His shorts were a pair of jeans hacked off above the knees, his sweatshirt boasted a faded picture of one of Cedar Point's roller coasters, and his sneakers had holes in the sides. He looked nothing like a successful developer about to conduct a business meeting. The man was an iconoclast.

He saw himself as her Prince Charming. She saw him as trouble. Four nights ago she'd lost all reason and had made love with him. Staring at him now, Bernadette knew any hopes she'd had of staying focused and businesslike today were lost. She shouldn't have come.

He smiled, his eyes the warm chocolate of dreams. His gaze was on her and only her. "You came."

"Of course we came," Tom said. "You should know by now that we're never on time."

Kat poked Tom in the ribs. "He doesn't mean us, you idiot."

"Oh?" Tom glanced between Cody and Bernadette, his eyes widening, then he laughed. " 'Scuse us, old man, we'll find our way in. You just go ahead and gawk."

He headed into the house, and Katrina followed, but first she spoke to Bernadette. "I'll look at those signatures later."

Bernadette said nothing. In her mind she could hear the voice of common sense telling her to run, to get in her car and take off. She couldn't have run if she'd had to, though. Her legs had turned to rubber, and air had ceased filling her lungs.

Cody reached out and took her hand, and she found herself inside, the door closing behind her. Only when she felt something wet touch her other hand did she look away from him. Sniffing her fingers, Thor wagged his tail.

"Must be he smells your dog," Cody said, and shooed Thor off. "You have one of those mysterious papers with your signature in there?" He motioned toward the manila envelope she held.

Bernadette nodded, words still refusing to form in her brain. She was beginning to notice things around her, however. People. Activities. This was no business meeting. Or if it was, it hadn't started and the participants weren't concerned with looking professional. She saw jeans and sweatpants, T-shirts and sweatshirts. There wasn't a suit or a tie in the mix, and at the far end of his great room, six of those present were playing basketball.

She knew then that she was overdressed.

Destiny Unknown

"You might want to take off those heels," Cody said. "I thought I said something about this being casual."

He might have. She couldn't remember. Even if he had, for her, casual attire for a business gathering was exactly what she had on, with maybe one exception. "I should have worn flats."

He laughed. "Do you own a pair of jeans, Bern?"

"Jeans?" She knew what he was getting at. "No."

"Sweatpants?"

"Yes, I have sweatpants." Two pairs, actually, for when she worked out. "I also have shorts." She glanced at his. "What do you do, wear your jeans until the knees give out, then cut off the bottom half and call them shorts?"

"Works for me."

"Thank goodness everyone doesn't think like you. You'd run department stores like Morgan's out of business."

"Well, today we're going to try to keep Morgan's in business. At least we're going to try to keep Morgan's general manager in business." He turned toward the men and women in his great room. "Time," he yelled, and made a T with his hands. "New problem to work on."

More than a dozen pairs of eyes turned toward them, and Bernadette suddenly felt like a fish in a bowl.

Cody took the time to introduce everyone there to Bern. Katrina and Tom waved when he gave their formal titles. Beside them was Bill Coplon, and he stood and shook Bernadette's hand. In spite of working with Cody for more than six years, Bill hadn't lost all of his CPA persona. His jeans were practically brand-new, probably donned only for these gatherings. Cody knew Bern would feel a kinship with Bill.

Henry and Gary, however, were her antitheses. Sometimes the two contractors disgusted even him with their disregard of personal hygiene. Nevertheless, they were the best around, and the work they produced was first class. Today they both seemed to have recently taken their monthly bath.

The couple who'd been doing his promotional work for the last four years came next. They were always interesting to be around: Tony with his colorful shorts and shirt, long hair, and nose ring; and Jenny, his wife and partner, who generally met the public. Not that Jenny was exactly conservative. Today she was wearing black leggings and a shirt she'd made out of the tops of aluminum cans. She called it a conversation starter.

By the time Jerry, who loved to cook as well as create stunning landscapes and gardens, came out of the kitchen, Cody had introduced all fourteen of the principal members of his team to Bernadette. Watching her reaction to each was interesting. She kept her expression carefully schooled, her smile polite, but her eyes weren't as emotionless, and they often revealed surprise when he listed the credits and the acclaim each person had earned over the years. If he achieved nothing more, he hoped she walked away from their relationship with some of her preconceived ideas shattered.

Then again, he hoped she didn't walk away from their relationship, and that they would actually have a relationship, not just the memory of one night in bed.

"Bernadette will summarize the problems she's been having the last couple of weeks," he told the group as everyone settled on the floor or in the chairs near the fireplace. "We hope Katrina can give her some answers, but any ideas you have will be welcome."

Stepping aside, he let Bernadette talk. At first each

Destiny Unknown

word came out controlled and precise. It didn't take long for his crew to start asking questions, probing deeper. Bill surprised them all by coming to Ben's defense, then he explained that he knew Ben. "Not that he'll hear anything about this conversation." He looked at Cody. "I assume the same rules apply here."

"Same rules," Cody said, and explained those rules to Bern. "Everything discussed during these sessions is confidential. No idea is stupid. Everyone has an equal say."

"Which is why I feel I need to speak in Ben's defense," Bill said. "He's not exactly happy about what's going on at Morgan's. I know that for a fact. But he wouldn't intentionally try to make you fail, Bernadette."

"You know that for a fact too?" Jerry asked, passing around another of his special treats.

Kat held out her hand. "May I see that letter with the signature that you brought?"

"Actually, I brought a letter and some ad copy. Both signed by me. Or so it seems. I know I didn't sign either."

Bernadette handed Katrina the manila envelope and answered a few more questions before Katrina spoke up. "Could you please write a few words, then your signature."

"What do you want me to write?" Bernadette hesitated, looking at the pen and paper Cody quickly produced.

"Two sentences. Anything you'd like as long as you use the word 'I' in one. Then your signature as you would normally sign a business letter."

Bernadette complied, and Katrina took the new sample, studying it for a minute before comparing it to the ones in the envelope. When she looked up, she shrugged. "They're the same."

"You're saying I signed those?" Bernadette's shoulders visibly sagged.

"No, I'm saying they're the same," Katrina said, and glanced at Tom, who had been looking over Katrina's shoulder. "You tell her."

"What she means," Tom said, holding up the two documents, "is they're copies. Computer copies."

"Computer copies?" Bernadette repeated.

Tom handed the letter and ad copy back to Bernadette. "They've been printed on a color printer so you get the signature in blue and the rest of the letter in black. I'd say your signature was scanned into a computer program and saved, and is being used whenever needed, shrunk or expanded to fit the document. The equipment is top-notch, the resolution high. It's a computer with a lot of memory and a quality printer."

"Ben has a scanner and a color printer," she said. "It's only seven months old. Parker bought them for him when the new position was created."

"And can anyone else use this computer and scanner?" Bill asked, still coming to Ben's defense.

"Yes. That was part of the justification for the expense. Loren, who's our art director, uses it a lot. He's in Ben's office almost as much as Ben. And anyone with a reason can use it. But Ben would know."

"He doesn't have any days off?" Tony asked, grinning. "Never leaves his office, even to sleep?"

"What did you find out about her?" Gary asked Katrina, popping open a soda can.

Katrina looked at Cody and so did Bernadette. He explained. "Kat's given each of us an analysis through our handwriting."

Destiny Unknown

"Would you like to know what I said about him?" Katrina asked.

Bernadette didn't want to seem interested, but she very much wanted to know Cody's analysis. She shrugged, and Katrina grinned. "His writing clearly shows a man who's confident in his beliefs and feels free to express his opinions. He's extroverted, demonstrative, and expressive. Impulsive to a degree."

"To a degree?" Bernadette had run into his impulsiveness, along with the demonstrative and expressive sides of him.

"Both of you," Katrina went on, "were strongly influenced by your fathers." She corrected herself, looking at Cody. "Or a father figure. You're also both strong willed."

"Tell me about it," Cody said, his gaze on Bernadette.

"Tell you?" Bern countered, then glanced back at Katrina. "He did tell you, didn't he?" Her laugh was stilted. "You two are in this together, aren't you? You're pulling my leg."

Katrina was perfectly serious. "All he's told me about you is your signature is showing up where it shouldn't, and you wanted a confirmation that it was your signature. Trust me, he didn't have to tell me anything about you personally. You did that in what you wrote here." She held up the paper Bernadette had written the two sentences on. "This isn't just a parlor trick. For years managers have been using graphology as a tool in hiring personnel. In France at least eighty percent of the biggest companies use graphology in hiring. It's all there—"

Again she pointed at the piece Bernadette had written. "How high the letters are, how low, their width, slant, and spacing. Even how much of the paper you use tells me something. With you, besides the influence of your father, or perhaps because of it, you need to have control in order to be comfortable."

Tom laughed. "And she got connected with Cody? Good luck."

They didn't understand, Bernadette thought. She had to explain. "Cody and I aren't connected, we're . . . that is—"

"She's my tenant consultant," Cody said, and picked up the basketball that had been placed in the middle of the floor while they were discussing Bernadette's problems. He tossed it to Bill. "What would you want if you lived in this new development?"

"Convenience," Bill said, and tossed the ball to Tony.

"Beauty," Tony added, and the ball went to Bernadette.

She caught it. Barely. It was that or be smacked in the chest. Once she had the ball, she stared at it, understanding she was to come up with a suggestion, but not sure what to say.

"Say the first thing that comes into your mind," Cody prompted.

"A front door." She threw the ball to him, glad to be rid of it.

Everyone laughed, agreeing a front door would be good. Cody added an idea, and the ball moved on.

Somewhere around five o'clock Bernadette realized she should have left, that they'd spent the last three hours working on Cody's project, not her problem. She should have left, but she was enjoying herself too much to leave. From tossing the ball, they'd gone to playing jacks—she hadn't done that since she was in grammar

Destiny Unknown

school. Next came a game of marbles. Her team won, then lost when they switched to badminton.

Each game was more than a game, and the term "playing with ideas" took on new meaning for her. Cody had created a think tank, and ideas were flowing. At six o'clock Jerry brought out more food—not that there'd been a lack of food or drink all afternoon—and a break was declared. Four of the men started playing basketball again, and Bernadette realized Cody's divisions in this room were purely functional.

Stretched out on the floor, she rubbed her feet together, her high heels having long ago disappeared. She hoped the shoes weren't being chewed to pieces by Thor, who'd been bouncing around with them most of the afternoon but had retired to a corner to chew on something. Her nylons were now shredded, and her hair had come out of its twist and hung by the sides of her face, so she had to keep pushing it back as she sipped the wine that Bill had brought to the gathering.

He sat beside her, offering her the last from the bottle. For a moment he said nothing, tasting his wine, his gaze—like hers—on Cody. Then he spoke. "What about Loren?"

Bernadette frowned, confused. "Loren?"

"You've been suggesting that Ben is doing this to make you look bad in Parker's eyes. What about Loren? He has access to the equipment, doesn't he?"

"Yes, but I didn't take his job. What would his motive be?"

"Friendship. He might be trying to get you out so Parker will put Ben back in as general manager."

"Friendship?" Bernadette laughed. "Those two fight like cats and dogs."

Bill's gaze drifted back to Cody. "Sometimes people fight to cover up feelings."

Considering she'd been arguing with Cody off and on all afternoon, she suspected Bill was no longer talking about Ben and Loren. "Cody and I are total opposites," she said.

Bill grinned. "If I recall, Katrina said you two had a lot in common."

People began to leave around nine o'clock. They'd made a start, had defined the scope of the project and the atmosphere they wanted. Much of it was what Cody had already envisioned, but the afternoon had produced more. Fresher ideas. New slants. It always amazed him. More than that, the afternoon had brought the disparate people together. Over the next three or more years, they would be working closely with each other. Now it would be in harmony, knowing they could disagree with one another and it would be all right. As they left, they left with pieces of the project. When they met again, the ideas would be more fully formed—architectural plans, landscaping, and promotional packages in their beginning stages. It would go faster if he did it alone, took control, but the results would be limited by his vision.

Sometimes you had to give up control.

He touched the gold chain around his neck and watched Bernadette play tug-of-war with Thor, the dog pulling on an old sock that had been lying around. She'd stayed. He'd even say she'd had fun. What she did next, however, was out of his control.

He knew what he wanted.

Katrina and Tom were by the fireplace. Someone had built a fire. Someone else had given the command for

Destiny Unknown

the lights to dim and music to play. It happened that way when they met to play with ideas.

Katrina glanced toward Bernadette, then back at him. Pushing herself up from the rug in front of the hearth, she walked over to him. Leaning down, she spoke close to his ear. "Want to change your mind about that offer of a bed? We can find a motel room."

He shook his head. "I doubt she stays."

"You've got a stubborn one there."

"Tell me about it."

"She can change. Changing how you write can change how you think, how you see yourself. I told her that."

"And did she believe you?"

Katrina laughed. "Not yet." Stretching, she looked over at Tom. "You ready for bed?" she asked him. "We've got to head back early tomorrow morning."

Tom took his cue. Bernadette also stopped playing with Thor. Awkwardly she stood. "I should be leaving. I never expected to stay this long. Poor Mopsy."

"Has used the papers you put down, I hope." Cody veered her off from her search for her shoes. "Have a minute more? I'd like to get your personal opinion on the project."

She laughed, craning her head slightly to watch Katrina and Tom start up his stairs. "You've been getting my personal opinion all afternoon. Did you clean all those boxes out of your spare bedroom?"

"No, they're using my room."

Her eyebrows arched suspiciously. "And you're?"

"Probably sleeping there." He nodded toward the rug in front of the fireplace.

"On the floor?"

"Unless you're inviting me to your place."

"No . . . but— I've got to go." She started looking for her shoes again.

He grabbed her hand, drawing her with him to the fireplace. "Sit and talk with me for a moment."

"I can't stay," she said, but didn't resist when he sank down to the rug in front of the hearth, bringing her with him.

"So what did you think?" he asked. "Will this be a place you'd want to live in?"

"The project?" She considered the idea. "If you put it together the way you were talking about today, yes."

She wasn't pulling away, but she was keeping a distance between them, her back straight.

"And what about your problems?" he persisted. "Did we solve them?"

"It's good to know how my signatures are getting on all of these cancellations and authorizations. And maybe Bill was right, maybe I should consider Loren as a possibility. I hope he won't tell Ben what I said today."

"Bill's a bit stuffy, but I trust him completely. If he said he won't say anything, he won't." Cody edged closer, and Bernadette glanced at the stairs. He understood. "They won't be coming back down tonight."

"I really should be going." Her look left him hoping, though, and she didn't move.

"I liked the way you blended in." He blended a touch with a light kiss on her cheek.

"They . . . I—" She stopped, her breathing shallow and her lips slightly parted, inviting.

"They liked you." Even Thor did. The dog lay near her feet, watching her with adoring eyes.

"I liked them." Her gaze played over his face.

"And me?" He brushed another kiss across her cheek.

Destiny Unknown

"This isn't fair." She touched his shoulder, but didn't push him away. Just the opposite. Her fingers curled into his sweatshirt.

He grazed her lips with his next kiss, then spoke into the empty room. "Lights out."

The lights went out, only the glow of the embers in the fireplace picking up the shadows of his features. Bernadette knew what she was doing. Though she'd had several glasses of wine, she was perfectly sober. Maybe she'd known all along that this was how the day would end. The protests had been to sooth her conscience. Her defeat would sooth the ache Cody created inside her every time he looked at her.

Maybe a second time would end the longing and expose him as just another man. She was prepared this time, would expect the rush. The first time was always special, she rationalized, though she couldn't remember a first time ever being quite that special.

He continued teasing her mouth with kisses, touching her face with his fingertips, and murmuring words she couldn't understand. The fire in the fireplace was going out. The one Cody was building in her was roaring, melting her resistance until she was touching him, combing her fingers through his hair to feel its coarse thickness and wavy body. He nibbled her neck and she nibbled his earlobe, playing with his earrings. One by one, he released the buttons of her blouse, spreading it apart and caressing her ribs before stroking her breasts.

The rhythm of their breathing became more rapid, echoing the frenzy of their actions. Her blouse and bra were cast aside, his sweatshirt stripped over his head. He buried his face against her breasts, sucking and squeezing, and she rubbed her palms over his chest, feeling the beat of his heart and the spring of the hairs that tapered to his shorts.

He was the one who pulled off her slacks. She was sure of that. Which of them took off his cutoffs was a question. Not that she cared. All she wanted was to feel his body against hers, touching, heating. Filling.

Underwear went next, her shredded nylons a waste anyway. Naked, they explored the unknown, tasting and melding until boundaries were forgotten, only the pursuit of pleasure motivating their actions. Not until Cody was on top of her, hard against her belly, did his groan penetrate her frenzy.

"I don't have anything," he said, a tension radiating from him to her. "Everything's up in my bedroom."

Bernadette understood. She also knew about control and planning ahead. She knew how brief happiness could be, how men came and went, and if you didn't grab on, you might never know any happiness. "I don't care," she said, and moved her hips so that he had no choice.

TWELVE

Cody clung to Bernadette long after the last tremor shook his body. The driving need had eased, but not the longing. Emotions long forgotten thrummed through his veins. As a child, he'd wanted to be loved. Unconditionally and without censure.

It came at times, infrequent times he would never forget. In those moments he'd soared, had thought nothing could be better. Now he knew he'd been wrong.

Loving Bernadette produced a euphoria beyond the emotions of a child, beyond the emotions of a young man. Looking back, he understood the mistake he'd made in marrying Bev. He'd been looking for his sister. Guilt, rather than love, had ruled his feelings when he was twenty-two. He'd thought he could learn to love Bev, thought he could help. He'd been wrong about that too.

I love you. Simple words for something so complex. Words that would petrify Bernadette if he spoke them aloud, so he remained silent.

He certainly hadn't planned on falling in love with

her. It had happened too quickly, otherwise he might have seen it coming and taken shelter. If this were a fairy tale, all would end well now. The spell would be broken, the ugliness that had scarred the princess would magically disappear. She would love him as he loved her, and the book would be closed.

Bernadette's eyes were closed and Cody waited, aware of every breath she took. Waited for her to rationalize away what they'd just shared. Waited for her fears of abandonment to resurface and take control.

The qualities he loved in her would be their destruction. She was self-sufficient and emotionally strong. Quick-witted and smart enough to know when to remain silent. Her silence held him dangling, unable to counter her fears even as they were tearing them apart. She was his princess, beautiful, regal, and wise, but she was also a woman, vulnerable and insecure. As she stirred in his arms he knew the fears were winning out.

Golden lashes fluttered, lifting to reveal pools of cerulean blue. In silence she scanned his face, her expression of pleasure slowly fading to dismay. Her body tensed, but not with the ecstasy they'd known just a short while ago, and he knew the next climax they shared would hurt rather than satisfy. She tried to pull back, and he resisted, afraid to let go.

"I've got to leave," she said softly, no longer looking him in the eyes.

"Stay."

"I can't."

"We need to talk." To say with words what their bodies spoke so beautifully. If only he could find the words.

"Oh, Cody." She sighed, nuzzling him for a moment, the resistance gone. Then she again tensed, drawing back, her nose wrinkling in distaste. "Did you just. . . ?"

He smelled it, too, the odor disgusting and sickening. Releasing his hold on Bernadette, he groaned and looked at his dog. "Thor?"

From his prone position on the floor, Thor lifted his head slightly and thumped his tail.

"Outside," Cody ordered, and rose to his feet, pointing toward the door.

Bernadette watched Cody let his dog out. Strewn around her was their clothing. It didn't seem to bother Cody that he was stark naked. He walked across the room as if he were wearing the finest of clothing, and she had to admit, he had a body to be proud of. He was the warrior, lean and muscular. The stallion, his flowing mane and bold carriage proclaiming his dominance.

He was also a man, and when he came back toward her, his gaze on her body, she knew his testosterone was kicking in again. Quickly she grabbed for her underpants. "I really have to go now."

He shook his head. "Now you know why I don't sleep with Thor. No matter what I feed him, and I've tried every brand of dog food available, including some Jim has recommended, that dog comes out with those malodorous reminders of his gastrointestinal functions."

Fancy words for what she'd smelled, but she knew what Cody was doing. A discussion about Thor's farts would distract her, make her forget she had to leave. A pause on her part would be all he needed. She reached for her slacks.

"So, what do you think?" Cody asked. "Is it Ben or is it Loren trying to make you look bad?"

Bernadette paused and watched him near.

Is it Ben or is it Loren trying to make you look bad? The question played through her head, and Bernadette stared at the doodles on her paper. If she knew the answer to that question, life would be easier.

Who was she kidding? She dropped her pen back onto her desk and stared at her closed office door. Life would not be easier until she made some décisions about Cody.

"Give us time," he'd said before finally walking her to her car early Sunday morning. "Forget what you should or shouldn't do or that I might leave. Forget trying to control your emotions."

Bernadette grinned. She certainly hadn't controlled her emotions that night. In fact, if she'd exercised a little control, she wouldn't have gone to Cody's in the first place, wouldn't have stayed until they were alone, and certainly wouldn't have made love with him half the night with absolutely no protection.

Oh, she'd forgotten control, all right. Now she wasn't sure what to do. Should she keep avoiding him, as she had been doing the last four days, or face him and try to explain, once again, why sex wasn't enough and it was for his sake that she didn't want to see him?

The messages he kept leaving on her answering machine at home and voice mail at work proved he didn't see things as she did. Why he thought she liked dogs, she wasn't sure. She'd told him she didn't. And calling their arguments discussions and saying she was perfect for him was a laugh. He simply wasn't paying attention, or he would surely see her faults. Even their philosophies of life differed. What he had long ago turned his back on, she wanted.

Destiny Unknown

"You're thinking in black and white," he'd argued Saturday night. "Sometimes it's not that clear. Sometimes things aren't what you think."

He was right about things not being clear. Everything was murky, in her life and in her job. Another three weeks and Parker would be back. Before he returned, she had to have things figured out. When starting a business, you needed a plan. Well, this was a business—monkey business—and she needed a plan to stop it. Picking up the phone, she rang Anne's extension. "Have someone from Security come up to my office right away," she said, a new determination to her tone. "Carl, if possible."

Cody stood beside Anne's desk, and she smiled at him as she hung up the phone. "Must be she heard me arguing with you. She's asked me to call Security. I told you she doesn't want to see you."

"Well, if I'm going to be thrown out, I might as well be thrown out of her office as standing out here." He started for Bernadette's door.

"But she doesn't want to see you," Anne called after him, standing.

He grinned and turned the knob. "So you've said. You'd better call Security."

He stepped into Bernadette's office, not quite sure what to expect. Her surprised expression took him off guard. "What are you doing here?" she asked, her pen poised over a pad of paper.

"Trying to see you." He closed the door behind him. "As long as you've called Security on me, I'm going to grab what time I can."

"I didn't call Security on you. I—" She allowed just a

touch of a grin. "Had I known you were out there, I might have called Security on you, but this is for something else." She waved the pen at him. "I know you said to sit tight and wait, but I've decided I have to take action. Starting today, I'm beefing up security. We're going to catch these damned shoplifters, even if I have to patrol the floors myself. And I'm closing that account at True Fidelity. Maybe I didn't open it, but the longer it stays open, the more culpable I become. And after that, I'm going into Ben's computer, and I'm going to find that signature of mine."

"And then what?" Cody asked. "Accuse Ben? What if Bill was right, and Loren's using Ben's computer? How are you going to know or prove it one way or the other?"

"I'll—" She hesitated. "Isn't there something in the computer that shows who was using it when a document was created?"

"Only if the computer's set up to identify each user." Bernadette's nemesis might have foolishly left the file under his name. He might have also left another identifying mark. "Do you still have those letters you brought to my place Saturday?"

"Yes." She rose and went to a file cabinet. From the top drawer, she pulled a manila envelope. "Actually, there are three things with my scanned signature in here now. Frank did give me the signature card, after making a copy for his files."

"Good. Now we just have to get Ben's and Loren's fingerprints."

"Fingerprints?"

Cody nodded, stepping closer. "And yours, of course. I have a friend who plays around with identifying fingerprints."

Destiny Unknown

"You have friends who do a lot of unusual things."

"Pays to have friends. This one, I think, may be connected with the FBI, though he's never said that, and I'm not asking. If you saw him, you'd think he was a bum."

"I thought that the first time I saw you." She glanced at his jeans. "You've dressed up today. Brown jeans. No holes in the knees. Brown sweatshirt. Even brown boots. My, my. A matching ensemble."

"See, you're learnin' me." He brushed a finger over her cheek. "You've also been avoiding me."

"I've been, ah—" She looked down.

"Avoiding me," he repeated. They both knew the truth.

When her gaze again met his, she straightened her shoulders. "It's really for the best."

He would never understand women, Cody thought. His mother had said the same thing before marrying his stepfather. Cody didn't find that arrangement for the best, certainly not for him. His sister had claimed it would be better if she were dead. He didn't agree with her either. Even Bev had used that excuse. On one of her sober days she'd said a divorce would be for the best for both of them. She was the closest to right.

"How can my not seeing you be for the best?" he asked Bernadette. "I don't know about you, but I'm at my best when I'm with you, when I know I'm going to see you. When I'm making love with you."

Once again she looked away.

"I know we're different." He brushed his hand down the sleeve of her cocoa-colored jacket, and her gaze followed its path. Their choices of colors were the same that day, yet there was a vast difference. "You like designer clothes, control, and organization. Actually, I'm fairly organized, believe it or not. And maybe I do need to dress up a little. I suppose I could do that. I'll buy my clothes at Morgan's. Be a walking advertisement."

She shook her head, a plea in her eyes. "You don't understand."

"No, I don't. I don't understand why you won't give us a chance."

"Oh, Cody." The whispered words were filled with pain.

"I love you." The words came out, softly and with feeling. "I can't promise a 'happy ever after' ending, but I sure can try. I'm steadfast and loyal. I like a lot of the things you like. I even have a couple of dollars in the bank."

She closed her eyes, and he knew he hadn't vanquished her fears. She wouldn't let herself believe him. If only she'd stop trying to control her emotions, would simply give in.

She jerked in surprise when someone knocked on her door. She looked at him first, then at the door. "Yes?" she called, a slight tremor to the word.

Cody remembered the security guard at the same time that Carl identified himself. Time had run out, and Cody stepped back. "I'll be going." He took the envelope from her hand. "I'll let you know what my friend finds."

Bernadette looked at her hands. "You wanted my fingerprints."

"Actually, I should have them on this envelope. Why don't you hold off on checking that computer until I call?"

"Ms. Sanders?" Carl called through the door. "You asked me to come up. Do you need help?"

She nodded yes, but answered no. "Just give me a

Destiny Unknown

minute, Carl." Her gaze on Cody, she lowered her voice. "I know you think you love me, but—"

He didn't let her go on. "It's not a matter of 'I think' I love you. I *know* I love you."

That said, Cody left, letting Carl in as he did.

Cody called that night. His excuse was a question about the papers with her computer-generated signatures. He wanted to know who'd handled the papers. She remembered the one from the modeling agency had been passed around at his gathering. Everyone had touched it. She'd also had the ad copy from the *Press* with her that day, but it had been touched only by Katrina and Tom. That was, if you didn't include anyone at the newspaper office who might have touched it. The bank's signature card would be the one with the fewest prints, she imagined. Even then, she didn't see how fingerprints could be lifted from a piece of paper, not with any accuracy.

On the other hand, if it could be done and Ben's fingerprints were on all three documents, she would know he was the culprit. But if Loren's prints were the common denominator, it would prove Ben innocent, no matter what she might find on his computer.

How Cody got Ben's and Loren's fingerprints became clear the next day, when Ben asked how well she knew Cody and if she found him a bit strange. "He's not exactly your typical businessman," she told him, laughing.

Ben shook his head. "He asked me to take a look at a picture of a dog he'd lost—insisted I take the picture and look. Now you tell me why I would have seen his dog. He even asked Loren."

"He loves that dog." She knew that for certain. She'd also bet the two men saw different pictures of Thor, and exactly where they'd touched would be identified for Cody's unconventional friend who dressed like a bum.

By Friday things were beginning to look up. At exactly four thirty-five, Carl and one of the other security guards who worked during the day stopped two women leaving the store. On them they found two blouses, a scarf, and a bottle of expensive perfume. What they didn't find were any sales receipts. Ten minutes later their male companion was identified by two of the older sales clerks, and the police took all three away in handcuffs.

Bernadette was scheduled to work that weekend, which was fine with her. Both Loren and Ben would be off, giving her a chance to check out Ben's computer without arousing any great suspicion. If anyone asked, she had her excuse ready. She wanted to use Ben's scanner. It sounded good, except when she tried to get into the computer and discovered Ben used a password. She looked around his office, hoping she might find it written down somewhere. After she'd tried every word scribbled on his calendar, she gave up. Even the hotshot from Shipping and Receiving who assured her he was a computer whiz couldn't figure out how to get into Ben's computer.

If her signature was in a file, waiting to be dropped into another letter, it wasn't bothered by her efforts. Cody's idea of checking fingerprints was looking better all the time.

He'd said they might have an answer in twenty-four hours, but every time Cody called, he said his friend hadn't gotten back to him. After four nights of calls she found herself looking forward to talking with Cody.

Destiny Unknown

Once he'd reported on the status of the fingerprints, they talked about everything and nothing.

Mopsy soon learned that the phone ringing after nine meant Bernadette would sit, and that she could get up on Bernadette's lap. For the entire conversation Mopsy would lie there, content to have Bernadette scratch her behind her ears. Cody said Thor was as bad, lying beside him and begging to have his belly rubbed.

Bernadette knew what Cody was up to with his extended calls. Sometimes he was so transparent, he was amazing. She also knew she should cut him off, that letting him think he was getting away with his game wasn't fair to him. He'd said he loved her, and though she knew those feelings would only last a while, it didn't seem right to lead him on. Yet whenever she did try to end their conversations, he managed to ask a question that led to another . . . and then another. The last time she'd talked to a male as many hours as she now talked to Cody was when she was going with Parker. But that had been different. Then she had believed in love and forever after.

She had Monday off, but she went into her office around four o'clock. Loren was talking to Anne, and both looked surprised to see her. "What are you doing here?" Anne asked the moment Bernadette came into the area.

"I've got a couple of things to finish up." She looked at Loren. "How's that Web site coming along?"

"Good." He leaned back, resting a hand on Anne's desk, and primped a little. "Should be ready by the time Parker gets back. You'll have to come down and take a look at what I have so far."

It was a perfect opening for her. "I'm curious how you got Morgan's logo into the computer."

"That was easy. We just scanned the one we use for our ads."

"We?" She wanted to hear him say Ben's name.

Loren didn't disappoint her. "Ben helped. I understand you were trying to use the scanner this weekend."

"I had something I wanted to copy into a file, but I couldn't get into the computer. You and Ben need to give me your passwords. What if something happened to the two of you?"

"We already thought of that." He glanced Anne's way. "Anne has them." Grinning, he pushed off from the desk. "Time to get back to my cell block. See you girls tomorrow."

Bernadette watched him stroll off, a wiggle to his walk. She'd noticed that he hadn't offered the codes to her. "I'll give you a copy tomorrow," Anne said.

"Thanks." Bernadette returned to her office, a sense of uneasiness hanging over her. Even after eight months she felt like the outsider. She could understand Ben's resentment, but she had hoped to win Loren over by now. One of them disliked her enough to want her to fail and was doing his best to ensure it.

On her desk was a report from STOPIT, the firm that had installed the EAS systems. STOPIT was insisting there were no problems with the surveillance systems in either of the stores, that the problems were within the stores themselves. Something was interfering with the radio frequency. Why it was occurring sporadically they couldn't explain. Actually, the report explained little; it simply denied guilt.

"Everybody's innocent," Bernadette said, and rested her chin on her cupped hands. Every time she went through the list of problems Morgan's had been experi-

Destiny Unknown

encing, one person came up looking guilty. Problem was, it was her.

The phone rang, startling her. Though she wasn't officially at work, she automatically picked it up. As soon as she heard Cody's voice, she was glad she had. That rich, whiskey tone was enough to chase away her depression. "How'd you know I was here?" she asked, noting her own voice had dropped a notch.

"Lucky guess," he answered. "Coupled with the fact that you mentioned last night that you might go in later today, and when I called your place, I got your answering machine."

"I'm not sure I'm glad I came in. The firm that installed our surveillance equipment reports that the problems we've been having aren't malfunctions but electronic interference within our stores."

"Well, I have something more interesting."

"Something more interesting?" she asked, hoping it was a report on the fingerprints. "Did you hear from your friend?"

"I did. And I have the report. In addition to your prints, we do have a print that appears on all three samples."

"Ben's?" If so, they had him.

"No, it's not Ben's. That I'm sure of."

"Loren's?"

Cody hesitated, then sighed. "That's the problem, I'm not sure about that. I thought I got a decent print on the picture Loren handled, but somehow I messed up. Listen, can you stay there for a while? I'd like to dust Loren's desk for prints, see if I come up with a match."

Bernadette almost laughed. How had she gotten to this point? In the last month she'd gotten involved with a man who was unconventional, to say the least; had enlisted the aid of a handwriting analyst and a man who might or might not be an FBI agent; and now Cody was going to dust one of her coworkers' office for fingerprints. If the situation weren't so serious, she would laugh.

"I'll be here," she said. She wouldn't leave if Calvin Klein himself came to town and invited her out to dinner.

After she hung up the phone, Bernadette leaned back in her chair. At last she was going to have an answer, regain control of her life and her job. The news was too good to keep to herself, especially since there was no longer a need to hold it inside. So what if Anne told Ben or Loren? Ben was innocent. Cody had said that. And once they had Loren's prints, they'd have him, whether Anne let it slip or not.

"We have a blue-light special," she said, stepping out of her office.

Anne stopped stuffing a letter into an envelope, her frown and wrinkled nose indicating her reaction to the news. "Now you're going to use K Mart tactics in Morgan's?"

"No." Bernadette could imagine how Parker would go for that idea. "What I mean is, I'm about to find out who's been causing me a sales rack's worth of trouble."

Anne sat back in her chair, her look wary, and Bernadette knew she didn't understand. "Let me tell you what's been going on."

She told Anne about the bank account and deposit, and the report she'd just received on their EAS systems. She also mentioned suspecting Ben. "But he's not the one," she said. "I think it may be Loren."

"Loren?" Anne shook her head. "You're kidding. It couldn't be."

Destiny Unknown

"We'll know when we get a sample of his fingerprints."

"Loren," Anne repeated, shaking her head.

"I know, it's hard to believe. It's been hard for me to believe anyone here at Morgan's would want to do this to me."

"I imagine." Anne frowned. "You don't suspect me, do you?"

"Heavens, no." She didn't want Anne thinking that. "Never."

"I'm glad." Anne smiled and picked up the letter and envelope again. "Well, I'd better get this in the mail basket and my desk cleaned up." She pointed at the clock on the wall. "It's almost five o'clock."

"Quitting time." Bernadette understood. "I'll be in my office. Cody's coming by to dust Loren's desk for fingerprints."

Five minutes later Bernadette's phone rang. Once again it was Cody. He sounded rushed. "Is Anne still there?"

"I don't think so. It's after five. I'm sure she's gone. Why?"

"I'm down in Loren's office. I'll explain as soon as I get there."

Bernadette hung up, then went to her door. She might as well meet him halfway.

When she stepped out of her office, she was surprised to find Anne still at her desk. Everything had been cleared from the top, and Anne was spraying a bottled cleaner over the surface, then following with a brisk rub of a cloth. "What are you doing?" Bernadette asked. Desk cleaning was not part of Anne's job.

"The cleaning staff's been doing a terrible job," Anne said, spraying and rubbing. "Dust everywhere."

She started on her computer. "Dirt." Even her keyboard was sprayed.

"I didn't think they were that bad." The cleaning staff at Morgan's was much better than the one they'd had at the Fashion Mannequin in Chicago. Bernadette took a few steps toward Anne's desk. "You're really in a cleaning mood, aren't you?" Anne got the back of her chair and the armrests. "You want to do my office too?"

Anne stopped, staring at the door to Bernadette's office. "I'd forgotten."

Frenzied gestures were not like Anne, but Anne was frenzied. The spray and the rag worked in rhythm, a squirt here and a rub, then on to another spot. Lots of spraying. Lots of rubbing. Bernadette watched, anxiety growing in her with each spray of that bottle.

You don't suspect me, do you? Anne had asked. She hadn't. Anne had trained her, had been her friend. Anne had been with the company for eighteen years. Parker saw her as a mother figure. Loren hung out at her desk. Ben cried on her shoulder. Anne was the cornerstone of Morgan's, the one everyone relied on, who knew everything about the operation.

Everything.

"Why?" Bernadette asked, and Anne stopped spraying and looked at her.

THIRTEEN

"I don't understand what you mean," Anne said.

"I think you do." Bernadette took another step closer, wishing she didn't see the guilt in Anne's eyes. "I just don't understand why."

Anne remained motionless for a moment, then slowly set the spray bottle and rag on her desk and sank into her chair. When she again looked at Bernadette, she'd aged ten years. "It shouldn't have been you taking over. Parker should have either held on to control or sold to Austin-Hill."

Bernadette knew about the offer Austin-Hill, a retail conglomerate, had made a year earlier for the two stores. Parker had turned them down. "Parker doesn't want to hold on to control," Bernadette reminded Anne. "And he doesn't want to sell to Austin-Hill, not unless it's the only alternative. You knew that."

"But to choose you to run the business . . ."

The smiles were gone, the friendliness. It was disdain Bernadette saw. Disgust. "I never realized you didn't like me."

"Oh, you wouldn't. You came here so full of yourself. This was going to be your baby. You had great plans. You said it yourself. You were going to change everything."

"Because Parker wanted things changed. He's been okaying everything." Parker had said he was pleased with her ideas. "And some of the things we're doing are his ideas, like the branch stores in Kalamazoo and Lansing."

"His ideas were reasonable, extensions of what his father did when he opened the Twenty-eighth Street store. I taught Parker everything he knows about this company. Trained him in the traditions I learned from his father. He wasn't going off on wild tangents."

"What wild tangent was I going off on? What was I planning that was so terrible . . . so frightening?" She didn't know.

"Redesigning the floor space. This Internet business."

Bernadette shook her head. With all that had been going on the last four weeks, she hadn't even hired a contractor to start the remodeling, and she wouldn't take credit or blame for the Internet idea. "The Web page is Loren's baby. You know me, I'm a novice on the computer. And again, Parker okayed the idea."

"Because you told him to go with it. I was there," Anne said, pointing a finger and lifting her chin defiantly. "He would have stopped Loren if it hadn't been for you."

"That's the way you see it." It wasn't the way Bernadette remembered. *Things aren't always what you think they are.* Those were Cody's words. How true they were.

"I've worked here too many years," Anne said, her anger sharp and clear. "I'm not risking my pension on an

Destiny Unknown

upscale, big-city thinker like you. I tried talking to Parker, but he pooh-poohed my fears. You were to have a free hand. That's what he said. A free hand." Her voice trailed off, and Anne shook her head, her shoulders once again sagging. "I knew I had to show him, prove to him, that you were incompetent."

"So you waited until he was gone, then started doing things to make me look bad." How clear it was now. How cruel.

Anne looked up again. She was smiling. "Actually, I had everything in place and ready to go before Parker left. It wasn't difficult. I simply scanned your signature into Ben's computer under an innocuous file name, and used it whenever I needed it. The letters of cancellation went out before Parker's wedding. And you did sign that card for the bank. You signed it months ago." Anne's smile became triumphant. "It wasn't Ben who slipped something past you. It was me. If you had known enough to look for a file with your signature in Ben's computer, you would have found the e-mail I sent to Gene after Parker left. Not that you would have understood what it meant." Anne was obviously pleased with her cleverness.

Bernadette saw Cody step into the office area. Right behind him were Loren and Carl. The three stopped just out of Anne's sight, and Bernadette kept her talking, wanting them to hear Anne's confession. "So you expected Parker to come back from his honeymoon, see what a mess I'd made, and fire me? Then what? Did you really think he'd take over again? Go back to the way things were before he had that stress attack?"

"I would have liked that, but no, I had another plan." Now Anne's smile took on a malicious angle. "Gene Hill talked to me when he saw Parker wasn't going to buy into his offer. All I had to do was convince Parker to sell to Austin-Hill, and I would not only have a guaranteed job for the rest of my working years, I would get a raise and a bonus."

"So you became a Judas."

"I did what I had to do."

"Including nearly killing my sister's dog?"

That reminder caught Anne off guard. "Mopsy's eating that sponge was an accident. I had to get something from your desk. I didn't think about Effie's dog when I moved your chair."

"Yet you were responsible for those defective sponges?" Otherwise it was too much of a coincidence.

"I was responsible. But don't ask what was on them that kept them from absorbing liquids. Gene Hill gave me the spray. He said it was some kind of a chemical mixture that kept insulation from absorbing water. All I had to do was apply it to a few of the sponges on the sales table. I knew Ben would come to me once he started getting complaints. It wasn't difficult to slip in a couple more of the treated sponges so that he'd think those he'd pulled from a new box were also affected." Smugly she watched Bernadette for a reaction. "There wasn't anything wrong with that order. You sent back two thousand perfectly good sponges."

Bernadette understood. Once the company checked those returned sponges and made their report, she would have looked like an idiot. "And what about the EAS system? How did you get it to malfunction?"

"That was easy." Anne's pride in her accomplishments made her willing to talk. "A few years back, my son had problems with a neighbor, one of those ham radio operators. My son bought a device that jams radio frequencies. It messed up that ham radio guy, and it

Destiny Unknown

worked just fine on those EAS systems. All I had to do was wait until everyone was out of the store, then I would come back in and set it up near one of the units. Connected to a timer, the jammer came on at varying times." She grinned. "You don't know how hard it was to keep a straight face when you were moaning and groaning about them malfunctioning. And you did almost catch me one time." Anne nodded, remembering. "Scared the bejeezus out of me that night you were here around midnight. If you'd checked back of that cleaning van, you would have seen me. Thank goodness loverboy showed up and distracted you."

"What about the shoplifters?" Carl asked, identifying his presence and stepping farther into the area.

Anne turned, seeing the three men for the first time. The haughtiness slipped away, resignation and defeat once again taking hold. She didn't watch Cody as he walked to Bernadette's side, but kept her gaze on Carl and Loren. "I didn't have anything to do with those shoplifters, Carl. Honest."

"Oh, come on." Bernadette didn't believe that. "They knew which departments to hit, which salesclerks didn't pay attention. And disabling those EAS systems certainly made it easy for them to walk off with the merchandise."

"No." Her denial was strong, the fire of innocence back in her eyes. "I didn't tell them anything. I didn't even know who was doing it until they were caught Friday."

Carl only half acknowledged his acceptance of her story. "They wouldn't have had it so easy, Anne, if you hadn't been messin' with our security."

"Nothing I did was really illegal." Anne spoke with

conviction. "I sent a few letters. Caused a few inconveniences."

"The transfer of company money to a private bank account qualifies as a felony," Cody said bluntly.

Anne held on to her denial. "It wasn't a lot of money. I programmed it so it would only transfer a few pennies from each account. I don't even know how much was transferred. What? Maybe twenty dollars a day."

"Ten cents or ten thousand, it doesn't matter. It adds up." He wasn't going to let her off. "It also nearly cost Bernadette her reputation. All I can say is thank God the bank president asked me some questions before taking any action." Cody looked at Carl. "I don't think we'll need her fingerprints after all. I think it's time you took over."

"Anne?" Carl held out his hand.

Anne remained seated at her desk, her lower jaw trembling and her eyes misting. Carl walked over and gently helped her to her feet, finding her purse as he did. "Come on," he said, encouraging her to walk with him. "We need to talk down in my office. I need to write a few things down."

She looked at him, her voice imploring. "I just wanted Parker to see she wasn't the right person to put in charge. If he wasn't going to run Morgan's, he needed to sell. For our sakes—yours and mine. You understand that, don't you, Carl?"

"I understand." Carl paused in front of Bernadette. "Do you want me to call in the police?"

Cody expected her to say yes, saw her start to form the word, then she stopped, her gaze on Anne, and he understood. Gone was the efficient, ever proper secretary. The woman leaning against Carl for support was

Destiny Unknown

the one who didn't understand, and her arrest would be her destruction.

"Take a full report," Bernadette said quietly. "Get everything down in writing and have her sign it. She's not to come back to work, not until Parker's back. We'll let him decide what to do."

Carl eased Anne out of the area. Nothing was said, not until Loren spoke. "Thank you for not pressing charges."

Bernadette looked at him. "I never realized . . ." She shook her head.

"She's a good person. Really she is," Loren insisted, tears slipping down his cheeks. Unabashed, he swiped at them and sniffled. "I've known her for eight years. She's been like a mother."

"I know." Bernadette nodded, a sigh escaping as Loren walked away. Cody slipped an arm around her shoulders, holding her close. She leaned on him, and he felt the tremor of held-back tears. "I didn't want it to be her," she whispered. "Not her."

"I don't think she understands how serious what she did was."

"I . . ." Bernadette looked up at him. "I thought she liked me."

"You invaded her territory." He'd seen it before. Envy. The newcomer picked on by the established group. He and his sister had been the newcomers when their mother remarried.

"What is it about me?"

He sensed her fears. Understood them. "It's not you."

"Isn't it?"

"She wouldn't have liked you even if you'd been Mother Teresa."

"I come on too strong."

She wasn't listening. "You're a leader. Leaders have to be strong. Decisive."

Bernadette shook her head. "You lead by playing games. You build a team. I don't know how to do that."

"You can learn. I can teach you." He wanted to teach her, to be her guide and be guided by her. To discover the meaning of life and happiness with her. The depth of love. "There is nothing wrong with you. I wouldn't be in love with you if there was, wouldn't want to marry you."

He hadn't planned on proposing to her that way, and he should have expected her reaction. Shaking her head, she stepped back. "It wouldn't work, Cody. In six months you'd change your mind."

He didn't touch her, but he tried to hold on. "I'll give you six months to see I won't change my mind, if that's what you want. I'll even give you six years, if that's what it takes. But I'd rather spend that time as your husband, loving you and being with you."

"You don't understand." She pointed at Anne's clean, sparkling desk. "She saw it." Her gaze went to the door of Parker's office. "He saw it, though it took him three years."

"They saw where you didn't fit into their lives. I see how right you are in my life."

"You see a fairy tale, but life isn't a fairy tale."

He reached for her, then dropped his arms in frustration and defeat. "What can I say to convince you that I love you and that that's not going to change?"

"Nothing."

"Nothing" described the next three days for Bernadette. Nothing was the same at Morgan's. Anne wasn't

Destiny Unknown

at her desk, and nothing ran as efficiently. Nothing would take away Bernadette's memory of Anne wiping the fingerprints off her desk, of her glaring her disdain or of her being led off by Carl.

Nothing was the same away from the store either. She expected Cody to try to see her, to try to convince her to change her mind. At the very least, she expected him to pester her with phone calls.

From nine o'clock on for the next three nights, she waited, unable to concentrate on anything else, always a little tense. Even Mopsy waited, lying on the floor facing the phone or watching Bern pace the apartment. On Thursday night, as on the nights before, Cody didn't call, and it was after eleven before she started to bed. She was just putting down fresh water for Mopsy when the silence in her apartment was disturbed. The first trill sent her heart to her throat and squeezed all the air from her lungs. Straightening, she stared at the phone as it trilled again. Mopsy barked, impatient to begin the ritual of being held on Bernadette's lap and scratched behind the ears.

On the third trill Bernadette closed her eyes, biting down on her lower lip and willing herself not to move. It was after the fourth trill that the answering machine clicked in. She heard her voice and message. Then she heard her sister's voice. "Darn it all, Bern. It's barely morning here. You should be in bed back there. Where are you?"

Immediately, Bernadette moved, grabbing up the receiver. "I'm here," she said, holding the phone close to her ear. "I just—"

Effie didn't give her a chance to finish. As usual, she began talking a mile a minute. "I know I said I wasn't going to call, but remember how I told you I was taking

Parker to 'destinations unknown'? Well, you won't believe where we've ended up."

"Let's see . . ." Bernadette tried to guess approximately where they might be from the rough itinerary Effie had left. "Japan?"

"Nope. Egypt." Effie's voice became muffled, and Bernadette heard her sister call out, "Come here, I've got her." Then Effie was back with her. "We're at the dig, Bern. We're with Dad. Here."

Again, Effie's voice was muffled, then a familiar male voice spoke to her. "How goes it, Princess?"

Princess. Her father had always called her that. Cody always called her that. "It goes," she said, tears filling her eyes.

"Miss you."

"Right. I miss you too, Dad." She always had.

"Your sister and Parker sure surprised me, popping up out of nowhere. Even got me out of bed."

"You know Effie. She gets an idea and time doesn't matter."

"That's her, all right." He laughed. "She's always been a bit like me, whereas you've always reminded me of your mother. Even when you were little, you looked like her." His sigh crossed land and sea, flowing through Bernadette. "I hope, Princess, that someday you find someone you can love as much as I loved her."

"I hope I do too, Dad."

There was silence, and she heard him clear his throat. "Well, got to get off. Here's your sister again."

Bernadette heard him calling to Effie, scolding her for going off. Bernadette didn't mind the delay. It gave her a chance to wipe the tears from her eyes.

"So, how's Mopsy?" Effie asked once she was back on.

Destiny Unknown

"Mopsy's fine. Misses you." Bern realized once she'd sat down that Mopsy had jumped up on her lap. They were back to the same routine of ear scratching. She was going to miss the dog when her sister got back.

"Less than two weeks and we'll be back. Parker wants to talk to you, but don't you dare talk shop."

"I promise." Her father's phone bill would be astronomical if she told Parker everything that had happened at the store, and she wasn't about to break the news about Anne over the telephone.

Long after she went to bed, Bernadette stared into the darkness, thinking. She remembered her mother. Not clearly; she'd been only seven when her mother died. She remembered a voice, soft and sweet, flowing blond hair, gentle touches, and an air of serenity. Her grandparents had often told her she was like her mother. She'd been pleased. She'd never thought that might be a detriment.

Closing her eyes, she remembered something Cody had said. "I can't tell you why your father doesn't stick around."

Well, maybe she could. Maybe after twenty-four years of blaming herself, she understood. He left because of her, all right, but it wasn't something she could change . . . or wanted to change.

You've always reminded me of your mother. Those were her father's words. What was good was bad.

Mopsy curled closer to her side, and Bernadette absently stroked the dog's head. What she'd missed after her mother died was her father's presence. The queen had died, and the king had gone into mourning. The spell had been cast.

Cody heard Thor bark before he heard the doorbell. Lids heavy with sleep refused to open, and he willed the intruder to go away. He hadn't been sleeping well lately, not since last seeing Bernadette. If he'd been a drinking man, he would have turned to the bottle. She was driving him crazy. Still.

Again the doorbell rang, and Thor's barking became incessant.

"Dumb John, wake up."

The voice came from the computerized answering machine attached to his door. A sweet voice. Compelling.

"I'm an enchanted princess and I need your help."

Cody opened his eyes, darkness surrounding him. When he was young and his sister was telling him the story of the golden chain, Karen had played each of the parts. For the mocking brothers, she'd dropped her voice low. For the enchanted princess, her voice became sweet and melodic. Oh, how many times she'd repeated the story, trying to take away the sting of that day's insults.

"Cody—" The voice came again, and he knew it wasn't his sister.

Sitting up, he commanded the lights on. He found his jeans lying on the floor and grabbed them, pulling them on and zipping them up as he went down the stairs. Thor was still barking, facing the closed door, his hackles raised. "It's okay," Cody said, though he was afraid it wasn't okay. For Bernadette to have come at this hour, something had to be wrong.

Quickly he pulled open the door.

She stood in front of him, his enchanted princess.

Her hair flowed past her shoulders like a silken cloud of gold and fell across the sleeves of a moss green designer suit. Eyes as blue as sapphires and a smile as warm as a lover's kiss greeted him. He would have called her beautiful except for one thing.

Her skin had turned green.

FOURTEEN

Cody took Bernadette's hand, drawing her inside. "What happened to you?"

She smiled, the green on her face cracking a little. "I've been put under a spell. You can save me, break the spell, but only if you're willing to risk your life."

He began to understand. "And what, fair princess with the green face, must I do to break this spell?"

"Ahh. It is very dangerous." She gave Thor a welcoming pat on his head, and he wagged his tail, sniffing her legs. "You must sleep with me and ignore the words of sarcasm and snobbery that may occasionally escape from my mouth."

"This is indeed very dangerous." He led her toward the stairs, certain the reward would be well worth the peril. "And for how many nights must I endure this sacrifice?"

"Hmm." She pondered his question as she took each step with him. Just outside his bedroom she gave her answer. "I'd say three hundred and sixty-five nights times fifty."

Destiny Unknown

"Three hundred and sixty-five times fifty." Instead of the bedroom, he took her into his bathroom. More than anything, he wanted to hold her close and kiss her, but the green goop she had on her face wasn't all that appealing. "I do believe, Princess, that would make me eighty-seven by the time this spell is broken."

She grinned. "For all I know, it might take even longer than that."

"Some spells are very difficult to break."

"Very difficult indeed."

He pulled out a washcloth and turned on the water in the sink. He hoped whatever she had on her face was water soluble. "What is that stuff, anyway?"

"It's that facial masque," she said, looking into the mirror and wrinkling her nose. "The same thing I'd started to put on that first night you stopped by my apartment. Remember the green on my forehead?"

He remembered.

"I'm sure glad I wasn't pulled over for a ticket on the way here." She scratched the tip of her nose, and the dried compound flaked off in a green dust.

Turning toward him, she frowned. "Are you saying you don't find me attractive? Are looks more important to you than what's inside a person?"

She was mocking him with his own words, but it didn't matter. All that mattered was that she was here, green faced and teasing him. Here, by his side. He lifted the cloth and began rubbing the dried masque from her face.

A splash behind them stopped his cleansing job. Bernadette turned with him to look toward the whirlpool. Thor was floundering about in the water, looking wet and foolish.

The dog couldn't swim. All dogs should be able to do

the dog paddle. After all, why name a swim stroke the dog paddle if dogs couldn't do it? But Thor didn't know how to do it. Time after time, Cody had tried to teach him. In water, Thor was like a sinker.

Cody dropped the washcloth and hurried to the edge of the sunken tub. Kneeling, he grabbed the ruff of hair around Thor's neck and pulled the dog to the steps. Thor was scrambling out when Cody felt Bernadette's hands on his back. Half turning, he tried to look up at her, only to find himself tumbling into the water.

Bernadette squealed as Thor shook, water spraying out from his head to the tip of his tail, wetting her and everything around. Laughing, she looked down at Cody, then began to undress. Her shoes went first, then the green jacket and skirt. A Liz Claiborne suit shouldn't be dropped on a wet tile floor, but that's where hers went. She didn't bother removing her underwear, simply jumped in, dunking her face in the water and scrubbing her cheeks with her hands, turning the water around her green. Only when most of the masque was gone did she move toward Cody.

He reached for her, drawing her closer. Against her mouth he whispered his greeting. "Welcome home, Princess."

The end of March brought the hope of spring and thoughts of summer. Swimsuit sales had been picking up, and their supply of shorts was already showing a decline, especially in the popular sizes. The renovations were beginning: A section of the store was blocked off and SORRY FOR THE INCONVENIENCE signs were posted all around, along with diagrams showing the changes being made.

Bernadette stood with Ben and Loren near one of the signs. She'd stopped them to mention the customer focus group she wanted to try. In a way, it would be like Cody's gathering of experts. In the case of Morgan's, the experts were the customers.

Bernadette was surprised when Mopsy came running up, barking an excited greeting. For a second she stared at the dog. That morning she'd left Mopsy at her apartment. The last place she should be was at Morgan's.

Then Ben lifted his hand in a wave and Loren beamed a greeting, and Bernadette understood and turned to look behind her.

Striding down the aisle was Parker, and beside him was Effie. "We stopped by your apartment and got her," Effie said. "I needed to see my baby."

Bernadette understood. Now that Effie was back, she knew she would miss having Mopsy around. As for babies? The way she'd been feeling the last few mornings, she had a suspicion she would have one around in about eight months. Losing control did have its drawbacks. In this case, though, she preferred to think of it as a plus. She was not only getting Prince Charming, she was getting a little prince—or princess.

She hugged her sister. "Good to have you back."

Bernadette hugged Parker, too, glad things had worked out as they had. For a first love, he'd been the greatest, but for a lifetime companion, he was better suited for Effie.

"So, do you have everything running smoothly?" he asked, looking around the store. "I see you've started the renovations."

"I've started lots of changes," she said, looking at Ben and Loren.

The two men nodded, and Ben spoke up. "It's been

an interesting six weeks, Parker." He gestured toward Bernadette. "You made the right decision. And things are beginning to click between us, but I'm definitely going to have to practice up on throwing baskets before our next planning session."

"Planning session? Throwing baskets?" Parker frowned his confusion.

"Long story." Ben motioned toward the Shipping and Receiving area. "Come on down to my office and I'll fill you in on all that's been happening. We can talk, man to man." He took a few steps toward his office, then stopped and looked back at Loren, grinning. "Oh, what the heck, you can come too."

"Go ahead, make fun of me," Loren grumbled, but followed Ben and Parker.

"Those two," Bernadette said, laughing. "What a pair."

"You look different," Effie said, stepping back to look at her sister. She beamed when she figured out why. "It's your hair. You're wearing it down."

"I do, sometimes now."

"And . . ." Effie cocked her head. "You look . . . happier."

"I am." Happier than she'd ever been. "So tell me, how's it feel to be an old married woman? Did you have a good trip? Did Parker relax or worry about the stores all the time?"

"That first week was the most difficult for him. Every so often he'd slip and wonder aloud if everything was going all right back here. I even caught him on the phone the night before we were to fly to New Zealand. That was the first Friday night we were gone. He tried calling you, but you weren't home. I blessed you."

Bernadette remembered that night. She'd been at

Frank and Marian's house . . . then later, at Cody's. "I was out until late that night."

"Well, after that, Parker got better, seemed to almost forget the stores. That is, until we stopped at that one bed-and-breakfast and were told we could send an e-mail. My thanks to you and Ben for keeping your replies upbeat. The one from Anne was a little strange, however. Something about hoping Parker knew you as well as he thought he did. Did you and Anne have a problem?"

"You could say that. I'll explain later. I was glad you called from Dad's site. That call couldn't have come at a better time."

"It was funny, but being over there with Dad, I felt I understood him a little better. I know we were there when we were younger, but this was different. Dad and I talked this time, about how things were before Mom died and how guilty he felt about leaving us with Grandma and Grandpa, yet how difficult it was for him to be around us, how we reminded him of Mom. I guess you have to be in love with someone to understand. If something happened to Parker . . ."

Her voice trailed off, but Bernadette understood. "It would be difficult to be around things—or people—who reminded you of him."

"Yeah." Effie came back with a smile. "Enough of the past. You won't believe what Parker's started."

"What?"

"A book." Her green eyes sparkling, Effie nodded. "He's working on a mystery. He's using some of the locations we visited on our honeymoon. And you know what else?"

"No, what else?" Effie had always been vivacious.

Marriage hadn't lessened her energy or enthusiasm for life.

"I'm going to apply to Clown College again. In fact, Parker said I should keep on applying until they get sick of seeing my name and pick me. And then, when I'm a Ringling Brothers and Barnum and Bailey Circus clown, he's going to travel with me and write a mystery about a circus family."

"And what about a family of your own?" Bernadette wondered if Effie had thought about that.

"What about one? We've already decided we want to wait a few years before trying, get to know each other better. Then we'd like two children. If I do get into the circus, they could travel with us until they were old enough for school, then we could either move back here or wherever Parker wanted to go. I think he's going to succeed at his writing. I read what he did these last few weeks. It's good. So, big sister—" Effie grinned. "I think you're going to get your wish. I have a feeling in a couple of years, you're going to have full control of these stores. You'll have attained what you've always wanted . . . at least what you've wanted since Parker's father started filling your head with ideas about managing a store."

What she'd always wanted and what she wanted now weren't quite the same, Bernadette thought with some amusement. "Parker and I will have to talk."

"Did it turn out to be more than you expected?" Effie asked with concern.

"A lot of things turned out to be more than I expected." Bernadette glanced down the aisle behind Effie and grinned. Her primary surprise was striding toward her, all confident and cocky, and looking like a bum, as usual.

Destiny Unknown

Cody had on a pair of the new stonewashed jeans she'd bought in Morgan's men's department for him. She knew they were the new ones, because she'd tossed out all of his old jeans with the holes in the knees. Nevertheless, there was a hole in these, just above his right knee. And stains on both legs. She shook her head.

He held up his hands, as if to say he didn't know how the hole or the stains had gotten there. She could imagine. He was a man who got into his work. A klutz and a daydreamer.

He also knew where he was going and didn't mind a bump or a scrape along the way. He was willing to take chances, yet would hang in there for the duration. He believed in playing games, in fairy tales and happy endings. He saw beyond the surface.

Effie turned, looking in Cody's direction, and Bernadette wondered what her sister saw. Effie had never been a snob. Clowns knew the disguises used to cover hurts. She would understand Cody faster than Bernadette had. They would get along just fine.

"Effie, I'd like you to meet your future brother-in-law," Bernadette said, and watched her sister's mouth drop open. "I hope you're not busy next weekend. I think there might be a wedding."

THE EDITORS' CORNER

Spring is just around the bend, and we have four new LOVESWEPTs guaranteed to warm your heart with thoughts of love and romance. Make a new set of friends by reading these touching stories of love discovered, love denied, and love reborn, included in our March lineup. So sit back, relax, grab a LOVESWEPT, and help us usher in a new season of love!

Karen Leabo's *Brides of Destiny* series continues with **LANA'S LAWMAN**, LOVESWEPT #826. Lana Gaston finds she can no longer deny a fortune-teller's prediction when Sloan Bennett appears out of the thunderstorm like a knight in shining armor. She's never forgotten how it feels to lose herself in Sloan's embrace and his steamy kisses. But can a single mom surrender her hard-earned independence long enough to find her future in a street cop's soul?

Karen Leabo maps the territory of true yearning and its power to heal old sorrows in this tale of heartfelt passion and dreams that will never die.

Danger and desire make for a perilous and seductive combination in Janis Reams Hudson's **ONE RAINY NIGHT**, LOVESWEPT #827. Moments after Zane Houston opens his door, shots ring out and he tackles his pretty neighbor, Becca Cameron. Becca is shocked by her reaction to this hard stranger, and when more violence sends them running for cover, attraction gives way to white-hot need. He makes her feel brave and sexy, driving her down a reckless road; but if they survive the ride, will they dare admit it's love? Janis Reams Hudson entangles a desperate ex-cop and a spirited pixie in this story of heartstopping suspense and irresistible passion.

Max Hogan makes a living looking for trouble, but ever since his wife, Grace, sent him packing, he's vowed to find a way back into her life in **EX AND FOREVER**, LOVESWEPT #828, by Linda Warren. Grace insists that she won't be wooed or won over, but when they join forces to catch a clever con man, sparks explode and nothing will put out the flames. He promised her his love for a lifetime. Can Grace convince Max that forever would be even better? Linda Warren's latest story of a couple searching for a second chance is both deliciously sexy and irresistibly funny all at once!

Speaking of second chances, newcomer Stephanie Bancroft weaves a tale of shattering emotion and desperate yearning in **ALMOST A FAMILY**, LOVESWEPT #829. Virginia Catron and Bailey Kallihan had shared the worst that could happen—the loss of their son. Now the child is again theirs to raise. Virginia has struggled past her grief to build a new life, but would rebuilding a family with Bailey mean losing her heart all over again? Stephanie Bancroft poignantly reminds us of how forgiveness can rekindle lost love in this novel of stolen innocence and the power of hope.

Happy reading!

With warmest wishes,

Shauna Summers

Joy Abella

Shauna Summers   Joy Abella
Editor   Administrative Editor

P.S. Watch for these Bantam women's fiction titles coming in March. *New York Times* bestseller Iris Johansen is back with another heartstopping tale of suspense and intrigue. In **LONG AFTER MIDNIGHT**, gifted research scientist Kate Denham mistakenly believes she's finally carved out a secure life for herself and her son, until she is suddenly thrown into a nightmare world where danger is all around and trusting a handsome stranger is the only way to survive. From national bestseller Patricia Potter comes **THE SCOTSMAN WORE SPURS**, a thrilling tale of danger and romance as a Scottish peer and a woman with a mission meet in the unlikeliest place—a cattle drive. And immediately following this page, preview the Bantam women's fiction titles on sale *now*!

For current information on Bantam's women's fiction, visit our new web site, *Isn't It Romantic*, at the following address: **http://www.bdd.com/romance**

DON'T MISS THESE FABULOUS BANTAM WOMEN'S FICTION TITLES

On Sale in January

GUILTY AS SIN
by TAMI HOAG

The terror that began in *Night Sins* continues in this spine-chilling *New York Times* bestseller. Now available in paperback.

_____ 56452-8 $6.50/$8.99

THE DIAMOND SLIPPER

by the incomparable JANE FEATHER
nationally bestselling author of Vice *and* Vanity

With her delightful wit and gift for storytelling, Jane Feather brings to life the breathtaking tale of a determined heroine, a sinister lover, and the intrigue of a mysterious past in this, the first book of her new Charm Bracelet trilogy.

_____ 57523-6 $5.99/$7.99

From the fresh new voice of MICHELLE MARTIN

STOLEN HEARTS

This sparkling romance in the tradition of Jayne Ann Krentz tells the tale of an ex-jewel thief who pulls the con of her life and the one man who is determined to catch her—and never let her get away.   _____ 57648-8 $5.50/$7.50

Ask for these books at your local bookstore or use this page to order.

Please send me the books I have checked above. I am enclosing $_____ (add $2.50 to cover postage and handling). Send check or money order, no cash or C.O.D.'s, please.

Name _____

Address _____

City/State/Zip _____

Send order to: Bantam Books, Dept. FN159, 2451 S. Wolf Rd., Des Plaines, IL 60018.
Allow four to six weeks for delivery.
Prices and availability subject to change without notice.

DON'T MISS THESE FABULOUS BANTAM WOMEN'S FICTION TITLES

On Sale in February

LONG AFTER MIDNIGHT

by New York Times *bestselling author* IRIS JOHANSEN

Research scientist and single mother Kate Denby is very close to achieving a major medical breakthrough. But there is someone who will stop at nothing to make sure she never finishes her work. Now Kate must find a way to protect her son and make that breakthrough. Because defeating her enemy could mean saving millions of lives—including the lives of those who mean the most to her. ____ 09715-6 $22.95/$29.95

THE SCOTSMAN WORE SPURS

by PATRICIA POTTER

"One of the romance genre's finest talents."
—*Romantic Times*

Andrew Cameron, Earl of Kinloch, comes to America to forge a new life and suddenly finds himself employed as a cattle drover. Scrawny, scruffy young Gabe Lewis joins the drive too, sparking Drew's compassion. Then, under the grime and baggy clothes, Drew uncovers beautiful Gabrielle Parker acting the role of her life—to unmask her father's killer. ____ 57506-6 $5.99/$7.99

Ask for these books at your local bookstore or use this page to order.

Please send me the books I have checked above. I am enclosing $____ (add $2.50 to cover postage and handling). Send check or money order, no cash or C.O.D.'s, please.

Name _____

Address _____

City/State/Zip _____

Send order to: Bantam Books, Dept. FN158, 2451 S. Wolf Rd., Des Plaines, IL 60018. Allow four to six weeks for delivery.

Prices and availability subject to change without notice.